Death on Mt. Pleasant

Death on Mt. Pleasant

*A Mickke D Grand Strand
Murder Mystery*

A work of fiction

Steve McMillen

ISBN: 1537107054
ISBN 13: 9781537107059
Library of Congress Control Number: 2016913529
CreateSpace Independent Publishing Platform
North Charleston, South Carolina

I would like to thank and acknowledge Bill Venrick - Historian - Complier, Lancaster, Ohio, for allowing me to use his photo of Mt. Pleasant for the front and back cover of my book.

Bill and his wife Jean are historians and they have two books to their credit: *"A Place to Call Home"*, a 99-year history of a county children's home and *"Echoes from the Hill"*, a 122-year history of Ohio State's Boys Industrial School.

PROLOGUE

It is 7:50 Sunday morning as Sissy Adams arrives at Rising Park. She drives by the public tennis courts and Rising Pond on her left, where kids fish and feed ducks in the summer and ice skate in the winter. She fondly remembers cooking hotdogs and marshmallows over the open bonfire provided by the park staff. Across from the pond, she observes the ominous, majestic sculpture of Mt. Pleasant, a 250-foot-high sandstone structure left behind by an Ice Age glacier. At the summit, a two-acre domain of coarse sandstone rocks and trees awaits each visitor. The mere sight of it never fails to send an uneasy shiver through her body.

Instead of continuing around the pond, she takes the right fork in the road, drives up the hill, and wheels into the vacant parking lot of Shelter House One. A source had called her last night saying he had some valuable information regarding a story she'd been working on as an investigative reporter for the local paper, The Falcon Express. He had not identified himself or his connection to the story, yet she had agreed to meet him anyway. As she switches off the car engine, the Ohio State fight song calls out from her cell phone.

"Hello?" she answers. On the other end is the man she is there to meet. He tells her he's changed his mind about them meeting out in the open parking lot and tells her he wants to meet up on the mountain. She pauses a moment. Her history with Mt. Pleasant sends a coursed shiver through her for the second time this morning. She hates heights, and she is petrified of Mt. Pleasant. Nevertheless, knowing how important the story is to both her and the entire community, she ignores her personal fears and agrees.

Placing her cell phone back into her purse, she gets out of the car, locks the doors, and strides briskly back down the road toward the entrance to the trail that leads up the mountain. She notes how few people there are at the park this early in the morning. Most of the citizens of Lancaster, Ohio, this small community just southeast of Columbus, are preparing for church or already filling the pews. She knows that emptiness will change around noon as parents bring their children to the park to burn off excess energy built up all morning sitting still and quiet in church. Other visitors will pack picnic lunches and congregate at one of the two shelter houses, while others will play tennis, baseball, soccer, softball, or just cruise through to see the natural beauty of the park. Many will climb the mountain after the lunch hour just to say they did it or that they can still do it.

Once she reaches the beginning of the trail, she slows her pace and gazes at the reasonably short, steep climb awaiting her. She realizes, at age 40, this will not be as easy as it was in her teenage years. Motivated by the information she hopes to glean concerning her story, she begins the uphill trek. She begins her climb slowly but it isn't long before she begins breathing hard, and she can feel her heart pounding in her chest and ears. When she arrives at the first stone bench set off the side of the trail, she sits down to rest. She seriously thinks about turning around and going home. She closes her eyes and forces herself to focus on what she stands to gain once she reaches the top.

"It must be extremely sensitive information," she whispers, telling herself, "Why else would he want to meet on the mountain?"

After five minutes of rest, she continues her journey. Once she has gone about three-quarters of the way up and after a sharp right-hand turn, she pauses at another bench to rest again, during which she tries to build up her courage to proceed. She ventures on once more. Five very long minutes later, she catches sight of the concrete steps, that lead from the dirt and gravel trail to the summit about fifty yards away. She is breathing hard, her heart is pounding, her body damp with perspiration, and there is a throbbing pain in her side. She makes a mental note, half promising herself that if she makes it to the top and back down again without having a heart attack, she will join the local gym tomorrow and get back in shape.

After finally reaching the top of the cement stairs and the summit, she eases herself down on a rocky outcrop to catch her breath and to try to squelch her underlying fears. She scans the summit for the man she has come to meet, but just like the parking lot at the shelter house, she is alone. Her appointment is not here.

At length she gets up her nerve and slowly but bravely walks over to the railing to take in the awesome view. While holding tightly to the black-tubular single-rail barrier, she lavishes in the breathtaking panorama of the north end of Lancaster. Her eyes encompass the fairgrounds below and the racetrack where they filmed part of the movie "The Green Grass of Wyoming" back in the '40s. She allows a smile to flood her face as she takes in Mother Nature's magnificent bounty. She immediately feels somewhat relaxed and encouraged.

She is so engaged with the vista in front of her that she does not hear or notice the impending danger approaching from behind her. As she boldly draws in a deep breath of the clean morning air, she is grabbed from behind. Before she can scream, a large, dark, gloved hand covers her mouth. Instinctively, she tries to bolt and escape but she feels her whole body being forcibly drawn back against her attacker. He whispers into her ear, "You were told not to go forward with your story. You should have listened." She can feel the unnerving heat of her assailant's breath pulsating against her neck.

Even though she is on the verge of fainting, she tries to struggle free of the man's death-like grip. He raises a large knife before her eyes, and then brings it to her throat. The more she squirms, the more she can feel the tip of the blade penetrating her skin.

"Scream and you'll die right here and now," her assailant mumbles through clinched teeth.

Succumbing to shock, Sissy faints.

Feeling his victim go limp, the assailant removes the knife from her throat. Taking a Kleenex from his pocket, he dabs at the slow trickle of blood oozing from Sissy's clammy, moist neck. He hates the sight of blood. Besides being messy, it's impossible to completely erase once it permeates things. Awkwardly, he attempts to return the used Kleenex to his pocket as he lowers Sissy's limp body to the ground and rolls it under the guardrail to the edge of the rock cliff.

He searches her purse and finds a stenographer's notebook containing details about the story she's been working on, and her cell phone. He places both items in his small backpack and places his foot against her body. Sissy's eyes pop open. She stares blankly at him with pleading eyes. He smiles back at her blank stare, and pushes her over the edge of the mountain. He watches without any sense of remorse as her body plummets down the 30-foot drop to the narrow rock ledge below, known locally as "The Devil's Kitchen." After hearing the deadened thud of her body landing on the edge of the ledge, he continues watching as she topples the remaining 200 feet down to the boulder-and rock-strewn bed amid the trees and brambles below. Sissy is dead before her body reaches the tree line.

"You've written your last story, bitch," he whispers under his breath.

❧❦

The park staff noticed her car in the parking lot late Sunday night. They called a towing company and had the car towed to the police impound lot. The first thing Monday morning, the police ran her plates and called her condo and her office. Sissy could not be found at either location. The authorities organized a search of the park around noon, and discovered her lifeless remains later that afternoon.

The coroner performed an autopsy, signed the death certificate and proclaimed her death an accident. There was no evidence of any wrongdoing or foul play. The only strange thing was that her cell phone was missing. The police assumed her phone most likely fell out of her purse or her pocket and its shattered remains are in pieces somewhere in the trees and rocks on the side of Mt. Pleasant.

Chapter 1: The Classmate

It's late Wednesday afternoon in North Myrtle Beach, South Carolina, and I'm in my office on Sea Mountain Highway in Cherry Grove. It's home to my real estate office, my landscape office and my private investigation business. I'm trying to tie up some loose ends before I take off for a couple of weeks for a tour of the Caribbean with my salvage partner, retired federal judge Thomas Alan Cadium. TC has a possible salvage job to explore and I need a vacation, so I agreed to tag along.

I venture into my private bathroom and gaze at my, now lined, 45-year-old face on a 6'1" 190-pound frame. I think most of those lines have appeared in the last six-months. Yes, I definitely need a vacation.

As I return to my desk, Jannie, my office receptionist, calls and tells me there is a call on line one for me. "Mickke D Real Estate, this is Mickke D, how can I help you?"

"Mickke D, it's Jake Tracey, Lancaster, Ohio, how are you doing?"

Jake and I played football and basketball together at Lancaster High School. We also ran around together and even shared a few girlfriends if I remember right. I hadn't seen him, much less talked to him, in twenty years.

"Jake, good to hear from you. Are you in town?"

"No, old buddy, I'm back in Lancaster. How are things in Myrtle Beach?"

"Well, pretty good, but hey is there something wrong? Why are you calling?"

He pauses before answering. "Do you remember my sister Sissy? Well, she died about a week and a half ago."

"Oh, my God, Jake, I'm so sorry to hear that. Wasn't she about five years younger than us?"

His voice is weak. "Yeah, she was only 40. I remember she always had a crush on you when we were growing up."

"I remember her well. She was a cute kid. What happened?"

He pauses again, and then answers with a stronger voice. "Well, the police said it was an accident. I think she was murdered. She fell off Mt. Pleasant. I understand you are a private investigator down your way. I'd like you to come up here and look into her so-called accident."

I don't know what to say. I haven't been back in Lancaster for probably fifteen years. I went back after my stint in the Army, but I was only there long enough to get divorced from my first wife. My parents moved to Key West, and my brother and sister both live on the West Coast. I never attended any of my class reunions. I guess I just had no reason to go back.

"Well, before I answer you, tell me why you think she was murdered."

"She was petrified of Mt. Pleasant. When she was a teenager, she and some other girls were playing around on Devil's Kitchen and it started to rain. The other girls ran to get out of the rain but Sissy fell down and almost fell over the edge. The other girls abandoned her, and didn't tell anyone because none of the girls were supposed to be up there. She was on her own in a thunderstorm for more than two hours before one of the girls finally called the house. I went up and helped her down. As far as I know, she never went up there again."

I'm not sure how to answer. "Jake, I remember that and I see what you mean, but you know what, I'm supposed to go on a vacation to the Caribbean on Friday for a couple of weeks. Let me check and see if my trip can be postponed. I'll call you back as soon as I hear something. I'm so sorry for your loss."

"Thanks Mickke D. Say, did you ever get married again?"

"Sure did, Jake, twice. But I'm single now."

He sighs. "Some things never change, Mickke D. Some things never change."

"Yeah Jake, tell me about it. I'll get back to you."

I wait for a few minutes before calling TC. I would like to help Jake, but I'm not sure I want to go back to Lancaster. Shoot, it might be fun. I'll get to see a lot of old friends and maybe I'll be able to give Jake some closure.

I call TC. "Hey TC, I've got good news and bad news. The good news is I am really looking forward to going to the Caribbean. The bad news is, is there any way you can postpone the trip for a couple of weeks?"

"Well, I don't know. How good is your excuse?" I can hear the disappointment in his voice.

"An old classmate of mine from back in Ohio called and said his younger sister was murdered, but the police are calling it an accident. He wants me to look into her death."

"Mickke D, I thought you were going to get out of the PI business. Every time you get involved with one of these cases, you get yourself almost killed. Do you have a death wish or something?"

"Yeah, you're right TC, but how do you turn down an old classmate? Besides that, I knew his sister. I haven't been back to Lancaster in forever. It might be time, you know?"

"Okay, there's no timetable on this salvage job, so no problem. Call me when you get back. But whatever you do, be careful."

"Thanks TC. I will. Any new ideas about where Captain Swinely may have buried the treasure?"

"Yes, I do, but we'll discuss that on our now-delayed trip."

๛

I wait for a couple of hours before calling Jake back. One thing I learned while a first Lieutenant in Special Forces was if you have the time, never make impulsive decisions. Take your time and think the whole thing through. Instead, I make an impulsive decision.

"Hey Jake, it's Mickke D. Looks like I'm available. I need to get some things cleaned up here and then I'll head your way Friday morning. Should be in Lancaster between 6 and 7 Friday evening."

"Thanks, I really appreciate this. I'll book you a room at Shaw's downtown. Do I need to pay you something up front?"

"You don't owe me anything, Jake. Just pick up my expenses and we'll call it even. And if I don't get you an answer one way or the other, you won't owe me anything."

"Sounds fair enough." He laughs. "If I knew I was paying for your room, I would have said I'd get you a room at The Hampton Inn instead of Shaw's. Just kidding. Call me when you get here."

I think for a few seconds. "Don't tell anyone I'm coming. It'll give me a chance to nose around first before we tell Lancaster Mickke D is back."

"Good idea. Things have changed here, Mickke D. You won't recognize most of the town. Have a safe trip."

ॐॐ

Before I leave, I tell Jim, my neighbor, a retired FBI special agent and the person in charge of my private investigation company, Grand Strand Investigations, that he is in charge of the office, as well as my dog Blue. I ask Mark Yale, the guy who runs my landscape company, who like me was Special Forces and spent time with me in Colombia chasing bad guys, to oversee a couple of bids coming up while I'm away. I ask Jannie, Mark's wife and the office receptionist, to cover the real estate end of my business. I talked her into getting her real estate license not too long ago, so she will have no problem with that assignment.

Chapter 2: Lancaster

The trip to Lancaster is uneventful, but also very relaxing. It is my first time piloting my new Cadillac SRX on a road trip and it is fun. Of course, I have no idea how to make anything work on the vehicle. I can't even figure out how to play a CD. The only thing I figure out is the built-in GPS. It takes me right to Shaw's front door. I leave the South Carolina Lowcountry, the flat landscape, the marshy smell of the coast, and the massive live oak trees, and drive into the hills and mountains of North Carolina, Virginia, and the beautiful mountain scenery through West Virginia. I have forgotten how beautiful hills and mountains could be.

Jake was right about change. I notice quite a few changes before I even get into town. I can't believe it, but there is a new road from Ravenswood, W.Va. to Athens, Ohio, and a bypass around Nelsonville, and a bypass around Lancaster. I take Business 33 directly into town and the first thing I notice is that Lancaster Glass is gone. You used to be able to see the roaring flames from the huge furnaces right from 33.

Shaw's is located right off the tree-shaded town square in downtown Lancaster. It is *the* place in Lancaster to stay. The rooms are very nice and they have a great restaurant and bar. Casual elegance and the comfortable, welcoming style of a classic small hotel greets you as you enter the front door.

I call Jake after checking in and he wants to know if I would like to grab a bite to eat. "Sure, Jake. Where to?"

"How about pizza at the Pink Cricket?"

"Sounds great. They always had the best pizza, along with Kingy's in Canal Winchester. Do you want me to meet you there?"

"No, I'll pick you up in twenty minutes in Shaw's lobby."

⁊◦◦⁊

I almost don't recognize Jake. He has put on a little bit of weight and he doesn't look as tall, but there is one glaring natural feature missing. He has lost almost all of his hair. He is as bald as a golf ball with no dimples. After a handshake and hug, I blurt out, "Jake, what the hell happened to your hair? It's gone."

"Yea, it happened about five years ago. It just disappeared down the shower drain. However, on the bright side, I don't have to pay for a haircut. Wow, look at you, though. Still the All-American stud, I see."

"Well, I don't know about that. Some days I feel old and not able to do the things I used to do, and for the past year, every time I turn around, someone is trying to kill me. I hope things are a little bit more peaceful up here."

I usher him out the door before he has a chance to ask me who was trying to kill me. As far as I'm concerned, that's history.

On our ride to the Pink Cricket, I figure I'll start my investigation. "So Jake, tell me what you're doing, are you still married? Tell me about your sister. Was she married? Where did she work? What did she like to do, and who may have had a reason to kill her?"

Jake has a look on his face like, "which question do I answer first?" He tells me he is divorced and that he owns an insurance company in town. He then fills me in on the life and times of his sister. "Sissy got a degree from OU in journalism and got a job at the local newspaper right out of college. She was married for about ten years, and her husband died in a suspicious car accident on his way home from work in Columbus. They had no kids and she never remarried. She became the editor for the weekly newspaper magazine, *Fairfield County This Week*, and she was a senior investigative reporter for the paper. She enjoyed taking photos in the Hocking Hills and canoeing on the Hocking River. I can't think of anyone who would want to harm her. She never talked much about her job, but I think she was working on some big stories for the paper."

"You said she never remarried. Did she have a significant other?"

"No, not really. She dated several local guys, but she wasn't serious about any of them. She never quite got over the tragic death of her husband."

We arrive at the Pink Cricket, find a booth over in the corner, order a couple of beers, a large pizza with the works, and double anchovies on my half. I look around the restaurant and don't recognize anyone. I whisper to Jake, "Tell me if there's anyone here I should know or if someone comes in I should know."

"No problem, got you covered," he whispers back as he scans the crowd.

I think for a minute. "Tell me about the car accident that killed Sissy's husband."

"Well, let's see. It was about five years ago. Her husband, David, was driving home from work in December. He always came home through Pickerington, cut across on Allen Road to 33 and then on into Lancaster. It was around 6:30 and dark outside. He went up over a railroad crossing on Allen Road, lost control, and slammed head on into a tree."

"Why did you say earlier that it was suspicious? Were there any witnesses?"

"The reason it was suspicious was that David drove that road five days a week and he knew it like the back of his hand. There were no witnesses, but a woman came upon the accident just minutes after the crash. She called 911. When the police asked her if she had seen anything or any other cars on the road, she said she had seen a large, black limo coming toward her about a mile down the road from where she found the crash site. The Sheriff's Department searched the area but found no limo."

I reach for straws. "Did they check the car for any unusual mechanical problems?"

"Yes, they did and everything was working."

"Did they do an autopsy? Could he have had a heart attack?"

"No, they said the cause of death was blunt-force head trauma."

Again, I reach. "Were there skid marks on the road? Had he tried to stop?"

"Actually, there was a light rain at the time and the investigators could not be sure. They said they found quite a few skid marks on both sides of the tracks but most had been there for a while. He may have hit his brakes, but they weren't positive. Even if he had hit his brakes, it could have been for a deer for all they knew. What does David's death have to do with Sissy's death?"

"I don't know, Jake. Just trying to look at all angles. Was that pretty much the end of the investigation?"

"That was about it. The Sheriff asked the public if anyone had seen a black limo in the area of the crash and no one came forward."

"Do you remember the name and address of the lady who came upon the accident?"

"No, I don't, but I'll bet the newspaper has it in their archives somewhere." Our crispy thin-crust pizza arrives, and we chow down on one good pizza.

Chapter 3: Mt. Pleasant

Jake picks me up around 7:30 the following morning. He suggests we go to Root's for breakfast and then I suggest we go up on Mt. Pleasant and have a look around. Jake agrees but I can tell he is not looking forward to going back to the scene of the so-called "accident."

Root's Restaurant is located on the north end of Lancaster not far from where I grew up. It is a locals place and has a great family friendly atmosphere. It has not changed much from what I remember. Again, I ask Jake to keep me advised if there's anyone here I should know.

We are seated in a booth next to a table of seven middle-aged to mature old guys and one young lady who appears to be there with her grandfather. They are discussing some golf bets for an upcoming golf match at Valley View. I whisper to Jake, "That girl is going to clean their clocks later on today."

"And how do you know that?" he asks.

"Because she's agreeing to all of the terms. Did you ever take up golf?"

"No, I just stuck with fishing and chasing girls. That's why I'm divorced."

I change the subject while waiting for breakfast to arrive. "Do you have any idea what stories Sissy could have been working on at the paper?"

"No, I don't, but I think one of her close friends at the newspaper may be able to help you. Her name is Donna Walton Crist, but everyone calls her Dee Dee. She and Sissy were tight." He writes down her name and phone number for me.

After a great breakfast, we journey over to Rising Park. We arrive around 9:00 and start our trek up the mountain. Jake weathers the climb much better than I do. I had to stop twice to rest, while he could have made it straight through. I blamed my stops on the big breakfast I had at Root's. Jake starts laughing and says, "Remember the night we sneaked into the park and brought the Crook twins up here?"

"Oh, my God, Jake, yes I do. Judy and Peggy. Those two girls were scared to death. I don't know if it was us or the mountain, but they were hanging on to us for dear life. That night will be etched in my mind forever."

After reaching the top of Mt. Pleasant, I determine things haven't changed much since I was growing up and bringing girls up here. I suggest we sit down and rest. Jake agrees. As I am resting, I ask, "Remember when you, me, and Twanger Delong used to come up here and search for caves?"

"Oh, hell yes. Every time you would read that book *Forest Rose* we would all have to come up here and look around because you thought the Indians and the early settlers stored food up here and used caves to hide from each other. How many times did you read that book?"

"Probably three or four times. It was a great book written in 1848."

"Mickke D, it was fiction."

"Maybe, but there was an actual battle up here in 1790."

My mind starts to drift. I am thinking that since I'm in town, maybe I'll look around some more if I have time. It might be fun.

"By the way Jake, what happened to Twanger? Is he still in town?"

"Well, you know if you would come back to visit or come to a reunion once in a while, you might find out."

"Yeah, I know. My bad. So where is Twanger?"

"The last I heard he was in Florida, still married to Carol, has two kids and is an ordained minister."

"That makes sense. He was always trying to get us on the straight and narrow."

After a few minutes, he takes me over to the edge and shows me where the police think Sissy fell. He turns around and walks back to where we were resting. I venture under the railing and look over the edge. The view looking down scares me, so I am sure it would scare someone like Sissy, who was afraid of heights. I'm beginning to think Jake was right. Sissy would never have come up here on her own, let alone get close enough to the edge to fall to her death.

Jake starts to get up as I get close to him. I motion for him to stay where he is. "Hey, stay where you are. I'm going to look around for a few minutes."

He raises his hand and says, "If you find a cave, let me know."

"Very funny." I continue on my way. While in Special Forces, we were taught to look for things that at first glance weren't there. This is one of those times. It's been almost two weeks since Sissy's death so the possibility of any clues still being around are remote. I turn to Jake and yell, "Has it rained in Lancaster since her death?"

After several seconds, he finally answers. "No, I don't think it has."

I wave and continue my search. I go to the edge of the tree line and start looking for anything out of the ordinary. After about five minutes, I find the thing that shouldn't be there. About waist high on a six-foot-high bush, I see what looks like a Kleenex. I take a picture of it with my cell phone before picking it out of the bush. I notice several dark spots, which could be blood. I take out my clean, unused handkerchief and wrap the Kleenex carefully inside. I take great care not to touch the spots.

I continue my search along the tree line and then I move into the trees about ten feet and travel the same path. I stop about half-way through and look closely at what may be some matted down grass and broken twigs. I scan the area from where I am standing and it's a straight shot over to the edge of the mountain to where Sissy supposedly fell or was pushed to her death. To the untrained eye, there is nothing here, but to my eyes, I see a spot or an imprint where someone was sitting and waiting or where possibly a deer had bedded down. I back up about five feet and gaze at the ground from left to right and then right to left. The high weeds and ground cover had been disturbed. Someone or something had been there. I don't want to get Jake's hopes up so I keep my findings to myself for the time being.

I return to where Jake is sitting. "So, Jake, should we leave and head on up to Allen Road? I want to see where Sissy's husband died."

"Sounds good to me. I'm ready to leave." He quickly replies.

Chapter 4: Allen Road

As we navigate our way up a crowded and busy Route 33, I ask Jake, "Do you know anyone on the police force who I might contact about your sister's death and maybe her husband's as well?"

"Sure, Steve Reynolds. He graduated with us. He was the one who called me about Sissy. He is a detective with the Lancaster Police Department but David's death was investigated by the Sheriff's Department."

"You don't mean big Steve Reynolds, do you?"

"Yeah, he was in the Military Police while in the Army and when he got out he went to work with the police. Made detective about ten years ago."

"Wow, that's great. He and I had a lot of fun together while we were in high school. I guess I should have stayed in touch with everyone after moving away." Jake stares at me but does not comment on my statement. I get the point.

We make the turn onto Allen Road and proceed toward Pickerington. We cross two rather dangerous intersections before arriving at the railroad crossing. The two intersections we just crossed over seemed like more of a risk for an accident than this crossing.

The railroad crossing is elevated and one cannot see the road on the other side until you are actually on the tracks. As we drive by, Jake points to the tree that David hit and then goes down the road and turns around. "He was going in this direction when the accident happened."

I ask him to pull over and park the car. Just as we are ready to exit the car, we hear another vehicle coming our way at what sounds like an excessive rate of speed. Suddenly a red pick-up truck comes up and over the crossing. I can see at least two feet of space between the truck and the tracks. I hear screams inside the truck as it lands on the pavement. Jake remarks, "I guess the kids think it's fun to jump the tracks. I suppose we may have done that a few times back in the day."

"Not me Jake, I was the perfect child."

"Right and pigs fly." He replies.

We get out and walk up on the tracks. Jake points at the tree. "He came up over the tracks and then for some reason veered right into that tree."

"And you said it was dark at the time of the accident?"

"Yes sir, 6:30, winter, Ohio."

"And no snow on the ground, just a light cold rain?" I ask.

"No snow, no ice, just rain."

"So even though he would have been able to see headlights coming at him, he wouldn't really know if they were on the wrong side of the road until he got up on the crossing."

"So you're saying he could have been trying to avoid a head on crash?" A puzzled Jake exclaims.

"That's about the only theory that makes sense to me. I wonder if that black limo had anything to do with it."

"But the black limo was going in the same direction as he was, according to the witness."

"Well, Jake, he could have turned around, just like we just did and checked out the crash. Maybe he decided to cut and run. People do crazy things in a time of crises. I need to talk to that witness and find out how fast the limo was going."

Jake hesitates and then says, "I bet Dee Dee can get her name for you."

"I'll call her tonight. Is the number you gave me her home number or work number?"

"It's her home number."

"Good. Let's drive on up Allen Road and see what's there."

Just as we are getting back into Jake's car and preparing to leave, a large black SUV slowly passes us. The windows are all tinted and I can't make out anyone in the vehicle. The SUV passes slowly over the crossing and then continues down Allen Road toward 33.

A chill ripples up and down my spine. An inner wisdom makes me suspicious. I had a bad encounter with another black SUV with tinted windows not too long ago. It was not pretty. I ended up in the hospital and two men from Colombia died.

I look at Jake. "You didn't by chance see the license plate on that SUV, did you?"

"No, I didn't. Do you want me to catch up with them?"

"No, let's go on up Allen Road and see where it goes."

We cross over Route 256, which runs between Pickerington and Baltimore. Not much to see, just a couple of nice homes on the corner lots and then ordinary corn fields until we get to a creek and what looks like a new concrete bridge. Jake tells me the bridge is new to him and that he remembers the old one was not much more than a one-lane bridge. He says he hasn't been this way in many years. Large trees begin on the far side of the creek and the road becomes tree lined and completely shaded. Then all of a sudden, it's as if we just passed into another dimension.

Jake and I are in awe. Both sides of the road have either, brick or wrought iron walls and fences with gated entrances. They are not just nice homes; they are estates with mansions sitting on them. I'm going to guess the lots are at least five acres. What homes we can see are set far back from the road. We pass probably at least twenty estates, ten on each side of the road.

"Whoa, I've never seen these before. This is nice." Jake quietly says, as if he is afraid he may wake someone out of a deep sleep.

As a real estate broker, I am impressed. "I would guess a few of these are nicer than some of the oceanfront estates in Myrtle Beach."

We come to another rather new concrete bridge and the estates end, along with the trees. We come out of the shade into bright sunlight and more cornfields before coming to a stop sign at Route 204. I ask Jake to turn around and drive back through the *uptown* part of Allen Road. Just as we cross over the concrete bridge, Jakes says, "We have company," and then I hear a siren.

Jake pulls the car over and says, "I sure wasn't speeding."

Right now, I am glad I left my .45 locked in my SUV. I'm not sure if my South Carolina carry permit is good in Ohio. I'll put that on my list of things to do later.

Jake rolls down his window as the officer exits his vehicle. I look back and see a flashing blue light on the dash of the car and the officer is dressed in what looks like a rent-a-cop uniform. He looks to be in his fifty's and he does have a gun on his hip.

The officer, with gray hair and a moustache, bends down and asks Jake for his driver's license and registration. As Jake reaches for his billfold, I can't keep my mouth shut any longer. "Excuse me sir. May I ask what police, county or state agency you are with and why did you pull us over?"

"I'm Officer Fredrick and I'm with the Robson Security Company. And by the way, I'd like to see your identification as well."

Sometimes I tend to open my mouth and insert foot. This was one of those times. "Look Barney, I'm not showing you anything and neither is my friend. We weren't doing anything wrong."

Jake turns to me with a blank look on his face. "I'm not?"

"And furthermore, we were just out for a nice Saturday afternoon drive and you pull us over for no good reason. I want to talk to your boss."

Officer Fredrick gives me a stern look and rests his hand on the butt of his weapon before answering, "My first name is not Barney and we had a call about a suspicious vehicle in the area. The description fits your car. Now, do I see some ID and registration or do I call the Sheriff's Department?"

I think about it for a few seconds and decide I may not want the sheriff involved at this point of my investigation. I reply, "Okay Jake, give him what he wants," as I retrieve my license from my billfold.

Officer Fredrick tells us to stay put and he'll be right back. Jake looks at me and whispers, "Barney?"

"Well, you know, The Andy Griffith Show."

"Yeah, I know. I hope he doesn't figure it out or he may shoot us right here."

Officer Fredrick returns, hands us our driver's license and says, "Sorry gentlemen, this is a closely knit neighborhood and we are paid to keep it that way. Enjoy the rest of your day."

I don't want to alarm Jake but now whoever called in the 911 to Officer Fredrick has information on both of us. I am also willing to bet the call originated from that black SUV that passed us at the railroad crossing. My hope for a discreet investigation is now blown. I am now going to have to speed things up.

As we near Lancaster, Jake wants to know if I want to stop for a sandwich. I think for a moment and then answer, "Hell yes Jake, let's go to that White Castle I noticed as we were leaving Lancaster."

Jake smiles, "Some things never change Mickke D, some things never change."

Chapter 5: The Accident

Five years ago, Dr. Jon Spineback is on his way home from his satellite office in Canal Winchester. He lives in the exclusive Standing Oak Estates just outside of Pickerington. Dr. Jon is an MD specializing in pain management. He has another satellite office in Grove City and his main office is in Reynoldsburg.

Dr. Jon is 42 years old and looks like a wrestler or a competing weightlifter. He is about 5'10 with a shaved head. He is not traveling alone. In the passenger seat of his black Chevy Suburban is Sue Ellen North, the wife of State Representative Michael North. Also along for the ride in the back of his Suburban are hundreds of prescription pain pills: Oxys, Percs, Vicodin, and Norcos.

Dr. Jon's practice is lucrative but not to the point of being able to sustain paying for his lavish home, three offices, twelve employees, and his upscale way of life. So Dr. Jon is a pain pill dealer with an extensive and fashionable client list. Sue Ellen falls within that category, and he has her hooked on pain pills.

She and Dr. Jon have been having an affair for the last six months, which was the only way she could pay for her addiction without her husband becoming suspicious. Her husband had called her this afternoon and told her he would be working late tonight and not to wait up for him. Dr. Jon's wife, Mary Jo, a veterinarian, is away on a three-day conference in Atlanta. Tonight seemed like an excellent time for the two of them to spend some quality time at Dr. Jon's luxurious home.

Dr. Jon loves to text. He is texting his wife, with Sue Ellen sitting beside him, and just as they get to the railroad crossing on Allen Road, he becomes pre-occupied with his phone and drifts left of center. Coming in the other direction is David Adams, who sees the black Suburban as soon as he gets on the tracks. He reacts and veers right to miss the head-on collision. Instead of crashing into the Suburban, he crashes into a very large tree.

Sue Ellen screams and Dr. Jon slams on the brakes. He thinks for a few seconds and then makes a rash decision. He knows that if he is caught with Sue Ellen and the prescription pain pills, his way of life is over. He takes one look at David's smashed car, sees no sign of life, and turns the Suburban around. He drives back to where Sue Ellen left her car. They only pass one other vehicle coming toward the crash site. As he drops her off, he tells her to keep her mouth shut and gives her some pills. He then drives around to the other side of Pickerington and comes home off 204.

࿔࿐

Terri Gandy is on her way home from work and shopping at the River Valley Mall in Lancaster. She lives in Pickerington and she was purchasing a gift for her daughter Samantha. It's dark, cold, and there is a light rain falling. She hopes to get home before the rain turns to ice. She doesn't like to travel Allen Road after dark because it is narrow and people sometimes speed on this straight stretch of back road.

She notices headlights coming her way at a high rate of speed and she slows down as the oncoming vehicle approaches her. She is talking to Samantha on her cell phone and not paying as much attention to her driving and the oncoming vehicle as she probably should have been. The other vehicle passes her quickly and it almost looks like a large black limo. She just shakes her head and continues. As she approaches the railroad crossing, she notices what looks like a light and some smoke on the side of the road. She slows and sees the mangled, wrecked car of David Adams. She tells Samantha she will call her back, hangs up, and calls 911.

When the Sheriff's deputy arrives, the only thing Terri can remember is that the vehicle that passed her looked like a large, black limo.

࿔࿐

Three weeks after the accident, Sue Ellen North is a basket case. Dr. Jon is concerned that she is about ready to tell her husband and the authorities what happened on Allen Road that night. It is time to eliminate the only witness to the crime other than himself.

He read all the reports in the papers and the woman in the car who he passed thinks the vehicle was a large black limo. The authorities have been unable to find that limo. With Sue Ellen gone, he should be in the clear.

He has Sue Ellen check into a small out-of-the-way motel and then has her call him with the room number. He parks about two blocks away and walks to the motel with his bag of goodies. He foregoes any sex because he wants no physical evidence that she was with someone. He gives her pills and has her wash them down with vodka. Before long, Sue Ellen is woozy. He puts on surgical gloves and sits her up. He pushes more pills in her mouth and pours more vodka down her throat. Within ten minutes, Sue Ellen is out cold. He wipes the vodka bottle clean, places her hand around the bottle, and leaves some pills on the bed. He undresses her and fills the bathtub with warm water. He places her in the tub and gently pushes her head under the water. Her eyes pop open but she is unable to resist. Within seconds, she drowns. He wipes down anything he may have touched, grabs her cell phone from her purse, and leaves. He disassembles her phone and smashes all of the parts. He tosses the phone parts in different dumpsters on his way home. He deletes all calls to and from Sue Ellen from his own cell phone.

She is found the next day when the maids come by to clean her room. The cause of death is reported as drowning from an overdose. Dr. Jon is questioned because he was her pain management doctor, but the prescriptions he had given her were not the pills found on the bed or in her stomach. He has all of his ducks in a very straight row.

Chapter 6: Donna Walton Crist

Jake drops me off at Shaw's after a great late lunch of sliders and fries. I advise him I want to do some nosing around on my own for the rest of the weekend and I'll call him Monday morning. He gives me his business card and informs me to call him at his office.

As soon as I get back to my room, I call Eric Sink back in North Myrtle Beach. Eric owns a gun shop in the building next to my office. I ask him if my South Carolina concealed carry permit is good in Ohio. He gets online and tells me I'm good to go.

My next call is to Donna Walton Crist. She answers on the first ring. "Could I speak with Donna Crist, please?"

"This is she."

"Hi Donna, this is Mickke MacCandlish. I was given your number by Sissy Adams' brother Jake. Do you have a few minutes to answer some questions for me?"

There is silence on the other end of the phone. She finally responds, "Oh, my God, Sissy was always talking about you. Mickke D, right?"

"Yes ma'am, that's me."

She hesitates before answering. "I'm tied up right now, could we talk later?"

"Sure, you name the time and place."

"So you're in town?" She asks.

"Yes, I'm staying at Shaw's downtown."

"Okay, it's 3:30 now. How about 5:30 in the bar at Shaw's?"

"Sounds great, Donna. How will I know you?"

"Oh don't worry, I'll know you. See you at 5:30."

ॐॐ

I walk into Cork's Bar at Shaw's at 5:30. After my eyes adjust to the dimly lit room, I recon the patrons and I notice a hand go up from a table near the back wall. I stride back to the table and stop in front. "Are you Donna?"

Without getting up, she extends her hand and replies, "Yes, I am, but please call me Dee Dee, Mickke D. Sit down."

Donna Walton Crist, I'm going to guess, is in her early to mid-fifties, very attractive with a lovely smile. "So Mickke D, you're just as Sissy described you." Her voice breaks as she mentions Sissy's name.

Before I can comment, our waitress comes over. I do a double take. She almost looks like my ex-girlfriend Beverly. She is tall, has long legs and she has a ball cap sitting atop her long blond hair. She tells us her name is Michelle. I order a Heineken and Donna orders a Diet Coke. I watch Michelle walk away and then force my mind back to current events.

Donna remarks, "Do you know her?"

"Oh no, she just reminds me of someone." I quickly move on. "So how did Sissy know anything about me? I haven't seen her since I was in high school."

"Well, she kept track of you through the internet and newspaper articles. You can find out a lot about where people are and what they are doing in today's electronic, social world. Anytime she mentioned David's death, she always brought up your name."

Michelle delivers our drink order and then I continue. "So did she think David's death was not an accident?"

"Oh no, she knew it was an accident but she believed there had to have been a reason for him to veer off those railroads tracks and smash into that tree. She wanted to know why the accident occurred."

I am puzzled. "Was she still investigating his death?"

"Well, I'm not sure. She mentioned it occasionally but nothing specific about finding any new evidence."

"Donna, I mean Dee Dee, on that subject, I need you to see if you can find the name of the witness who came upon the crash that night."

"No problem, I'll be at the newspaper Monday morning to meet the new person in charge of Sissy's weekly magazine. I'll search it for you then. It should not be hard to find."

"So Dee Dee, what do you do at the newspaper, and how did you know Sissy?"

"I'm an editing consultant. I freelance with the newspaper and I edited Sissy's weekly magazine for her. I've known Sissy for almost twelve years. Her death was quite a shock to me." Again, her voice cracks when mentioning Sissy's name.

The rather quiet atmosphere in the bar is interrupted by a piercing sound from a microphone being adjusted. I turn and look toward the bar area and a guy is setting up speakers and a microphone. He rests his guitar against a stool and apologizes for the unexpected shrill intrusion. I check my watch; almost 6:00. I have a lot more questions for Donna, so I ask, "Would you like to order something to eat? I guess we could go somewhere else if you think it will become too noisy in here."

"That would be great, but we can stay here. That's Chicky's Boy, real name John Cubito, and he plays guitar and an occasional harmonica. He sings oldies but goodies, nothing loud or over the top. He's here every Saturday night from 6 to 9. The Rusty Walters Band is here on most Friday nights and they're enjoyable as well."

"Sounds good to me." I wave at Michelle and she brings menus with her. I order another beer and Donna just asks for a glass of water with lemon. We both order and then I ask, "Do you have any idea what stories Sissy was working on?"

"Well, I know she was working on a story about the oil and gas industry and how fracking might affect the environment, especially Lancaster's water supply. I think she was also looking into why Anchor Hocking was considering outsourcing its distribution center and possibly laying off many people. She was also working on something that had to do with pain pill addiction."

"Would any of those stories get her killed?" I ask as Michelle delivers our sandwiches. My mind wanders again as she walks away.

She gets a quizzical look on her face before answering. "I certainly would not think so. Hey, are you sure you don't know our waitress?"

"No, I'm afraid not."

We finish our dinner with mainly small talk. I ask her to try to think of anything or anyone who might have a grudge against Sissy and to please contact me when she gets the name of the witness at David's crash scene.

I pay the bill and leave Michelle a large tip. As we are leaving, I put a twenty in Chicky's Boy's tip jar and give him thumbs up. I walk Donna out to her car, which is parked in Shaw's lot next door, and thank her again for her help. I ask her not to say anything about me looking into Sissy or David's death. All of a sudden, she gives me a quick hug and says, "Thanks for being here. Sissy would really appreciate this."

I watch her pull out of the lot and then I turn to go back into Shaw's. Suddenly, I have one of those old Army survival feelings. I feel the hairs on the back of my neck begin to tingle. Someone is watching me. I go back into Shaw's as if nothing is wrong and quickly go out the side entrance. I reach for my chrome-plated .45 and, of course, I realize I left it in my room. I go around the back of the hotel and look for the black Suburban I saw on Allen Road this afternoon. I check the back and the side lot where Donna had parked. I see no sign of a black Suburban. I walk back around to the front of Shaw's and look for the vehicle parked along the street. Nothing again, but I do notice a silver pick-up truck leave from Fairfield Federal's parking lot across the street. It left so quickly, I didn't get a chance to see the tag number. Now I have two vehicles to watch for, the black SUV and a silver pick-up.

☙❧

When I return to my room, I call Jake and ask him if he has a number for big Steve. He says he does and gives me his cell phone number. I thank Jake and immediately call Steve. He answers on the first ring. "This is Steve."

"Well, how in the hell are you, you big no-good bonehead?"

I can tell he has no idea who's calling. "Who is this?"

"It's me, Mickke D, how's it hanging?"

"Oh, my God, Mickke D. Are you still alive? I figured some woman's husband would have shot you by now."

I can hear a woman's voice in the background. "Is that Sharon? Are you still married to the same lovely woman?"

"Yes I am. What about you, are you still married?

"No, I'm not. I tried it three times and finally gave up. Became too expensive."

"So why are you calling me after all these years of not hearing a single solitary word from you, not even a Christmas card?"

"Yea I know, my bad. Well, I'm in town and I'd like to get together with you sometime. Jake told me you are now a detective with the police."

"Yea, poor Jake. Did you hear about his sister Sissy?"

"Yes, I did. That's why I'm in town."

Chapter 7: Detective Reynolds

I make plans to meet Steve for lunch the following day. He suggests Tiki Lanes. He said they have a wonderful Sunday brunch. I haven't been there in forever so I agree. I used to work at Lincoln Lanes when I was in high school and I became a good bowler. Tiki was one of the places I used to bowl.

I recognize big Steve the minute he walks in the door. Big Steve is still big, about 6'2 and 250 pounds of big, square jaw, and an Army style haircut. After some trash talk and checking out the brunch buffet, we get down to business. I tell Steve about Jake asking me to look into his sister's death. He is confused. "Mickke D, why did Jake call you? There's not one shred of evidence that Sissy was murdered."

"Well, if that's the case, you won't mind if I do some snooping around to put Jake's concerns at rest, will you?"

He counters. "Speaking of snooping, I did some snooping of my own after I talked to you yesterday. Seems as if you have a PI business in North Myrtle Beach and you did investigative work while you were in Special Forces. I also contacted a Detective Concile with the North Myrtle Beach police. She actually spoke highly of you, although she told me never to let you know she said that."

"Well done, big Steve, well done."

He gets a very serious look on his face. "One thing we need to get straight right now. My name is Steve or Detective Reynolds. If I hear you call me big Steve one more time, I'm going to deck you, and you can tell Jake the same thing. We're not in high school anymore."

No one wants decked by big Steve, so I reply, "No problem, Detective Reynolds. So does this mean you are going to be available if I need some inside help?"

His happy face returns, "Sure, for Jake's sake I'll help any way I can, but I won't jeopardize my job."

We take our turn in the serving line and I continue my investigation over brunch. "So how do you reconcile the fact that Sissy was scared to death of Mt. Pleasant? Why do you think she was up there in the first place?"

He answers right away. "She was trying to overcome her fear of Mt. Pleasant, got too close to the edge, and fell. Or maybe she fainted and fell."

"Okay, so what about her cell phone? Jake said the police have still not found her cell phone?"

"That one I don't have an answer for. It could have fallen out of her purse and shattered on the rocks on the way down. We're still looking into that."

"Oh, so the investigation is not over?"

"Yes and no. We would like to find the cell phone if possible."

I reach in my pocket and pull out my handkerchief. I take out the Kleenex and show it to big Steve. "I found this up on the mountain stuck in a bush near the tree line. Can you check to see if it's blood, and if it is, run a DNA test to see if it matches Sissy?"

"Where did you find that? We combed the entire top of Mt. Pleasant the day we found her body. In addition, you know since you disturbed the evidence, it won't stand up in court. How many days have you had it in your pocket?"

"Just one. I guess I just got lucky. I took a picture of the Kleenex in the bush before I removed it, and I found an area where someone could have been sitting and waiting. Of course, it could have been a deer for all I know." I show him both pictures on my phone.

He looks at each picture, "Well, at least you took a picture before you removed it from the bush. I don't see an area in the other picture where someone was sitting."

"To the untrained eye, it isn't visible and you weren't looking for it. Oh, and by the way, I didn't tell Jake about the Kleenex because it could be nothing."

"No problem, it most likely is nothing."

"So, detective, one more question. Do you think you could get me the case file from the Sheriff's office on the death of Sissy's husband, David?"

"What the hell has David's death got to do with Sissy's death?"

"That's the same thing Jake asked. I'll tell you the same thing I told him. Just covering all my bases."

He shakes his head, "Why am I beginning to think that you covering all the bases is going to get me in hot water? Sharon told me before I left the house to be careful, that you would probably end up getting me in trouble just like you always did when we were growing up."

"Now come on Steve, when did I ever get you into trouble?"

He gives me a pained look. "Let me count the ways, Mickke D, let me count the ways."

I quickly change the subject before he starts naming people and places. "I do have one more request of you. Do you know an area just south of Pickerington on Allen Road with big lots and huge homes?"

"Sure, it's called Standing Oaks Estates, and it's a rather exclusive area. What does it have to do with anything?"

"Well, I don't know but I would like you to see if anyone living there owns a black SUV, probably not more than a year or two old. And while you're checking, could you see if anyone working for Robson Security Services owns a silver Ford pick-up, maybe an F-150?"

"Damn Mickke D, I thought you were the PI. Sounds like I'm doing all the work."

"Well, I'll tell you what. When I figure out who killed Sissy, I'll give you all the credit."

With a scornful look on his face he replies, "Let me say this one more time, Sissy's death and David's death were both accidents."

As we are finishing our brunch, a man walks by, recognizes Steve, and asks us if we enjoyed our brunch. Steve introduces him as the general manager at Tiki. Steve bowls there and from the conversation, I gather he is a high-average bowler.

I look at Steve. "Guess I taught you well."

"Yeah, right. You wish," he replies.

As we are leaving, I give Steve my cell phone number and tell him he can call me any time. I also ask him to put a rush on that possible blood sample and DNA analysis. He just shakes his head and walks away. I call out, "Tell Sharon I said hello." He puts his hand up and keeps on walking.

I feel much better now. I have someone on the inside with direct access to important information and evidence.

∂∾∽

Before returning to Shaw's, I drive around town for a while. Jake was right; there are quite a few changes since I was last here. I drive by Lincoln Lanes, but the building is dark. A sign on the door read, "Thanks for all the great years, The Management." I'd had a lot of good times there, met many nice people, and made quite a few good friends. It actually made me think about my first wife, since I met her there, but that thought did not linger very long.

Once I return to Shaw's, I write down everything that has taken place so far, what I need to follow up on, and what I need to do next. Just as I am finishing my notes, my cell phone rings. It's Donna Crist. "Mickke D, I didn't want to wait until tomorrow, so I started checking online and found the article about David's accident. The woman who came upon the accident was a Terri Gandy. Not much information, just that she lived in Pickerington and worked at Dick's in the River Valley Mall."

"Thanks Dee Dee, I appreciate the help. I'll check her out tomorrow."

∂∾∽

That night, before going to bed and beginning the book I brought along, I call Jim, "Hey, big guy, anything exciting going on at the beach?"

"Mickke D, it's the weekend here, probably the same up there? Say, since you're in Ohio, will you pick up some Ohio State T-shirts for me? Size XL."

"I'll see what I can find. How's Blue?"

"Oh, he's fine. I brought him over here to spend the night. When are you coming back?"

"Not sure. Looks like I have a can of worms up here. I'll keep you advised."

"If you need some help, let me know, and don't forget the T-shirts."

I get out my book, *Baskets of Eyes* by local Myrtle Beach author John Barry, and begin reading. Within ten minutes, my eyes begin to close, so I shut the book, turn off the light and fall asleep. I get lucky tonight, no bad dreams.

Chapter 8: Rising Park

I start my day with breakfast at Shaw's and then go out for a brisk two-mile jog around downtown Lancaster. After my not-so-great trek up Mt. Pleasant, I figure I should do some roadwork.

While on my jog, I notice several different businesses, including The Ohio Glass Museum on Main Street, which look interesting. I make a mental note to try to go through it before I leave town. I also have the feeling, again, that someone is watching me, but I am unable to locate the source of my concern.

After my shower and before I leave Shaw's, I call big Steve. "So, detective, have you had a chance to check out that possible evidence I gave you yesterday?"

My phone is silent. I begin to think the call was dropped. "Mickke D, I've only been in the office for an hour and a half, and you've only been in town two days and already you're becoming a pain in the ass."

"No, detective, I'm just following up on our meeting yesterday."

Again, there is a pause before he continues. "I did find out one thing for you. That Kleenex did have spots of blood on it."

I exclaim, "Yes, I was right! Is it Sissy's blood?" I know the answer, but I just want to rattle his cage a little bit.

"Oh, come on, you know it takes days, sometimes weeks, for a DNA analysis."

"Well, see if you can speed things up. I need to solve this case for Jake and get back to the beach."

"Very funny. Why don't you just go back to the beach and I'll call you when I get the results."

"Right." I tell big Steve to keep me advised and leave Shaw's to go to River Valley Mall. Since I know my carry-permit is good in Ohio, I take my .45 with me.

Upon leaving the parking area, I opt to go the roundabout way to the mall. I drive up Main Street, turn left on High Street, and head toward Rising Park. I am going to try to figure out if someone is following me. I turn right on Wheeling, left on Maple and left on Sixth, which takes me back to High Street. I turn right on High Street and by the time I get to Fair Avenue, my concerns are validated. A silver Ford pick-up, probably the same one I saw the other night, is still about a block behind me. He came out of Fairfield Federal's parking lot as I headed up Main Street. He was easy to spot, so he must not be a pro.

I drive into Rising Park and go directly to Shelter House One. I park my vehicle and go into the shelter house. From behind a stone pillar, I watch as the Ford pick-up goes to the far end of the parking area and backs his vehicle into a space. The person inside does not get out. I go out the back way and down over the hill toward the pond, jog up the road, which comes in behind the shelter house, and end up about fifty yards behind and to the left of the pick-up. I hope that the person inside will be concentrating on the shelter house and not looking behind him.

With .45 in hand, I cautiously move from tree to tree until I am no more than ten yards from him. I sprint to the driver's side window and point the .45 at him as I motion for him to roll down his window.

Terror grips his face as he slowly rolls down the window. I press the .45 against his ear and ask, "Do you know what this is?" He nods his head. "Do you know how it works?" He agrees again. "I pull the hammer back." He hears the click. "And then I pull the trigger and you die." He closes his eyes tightly.

He finally moans, "Oh, please don't shoot me."

I open his door and pull him out. I can tell by the look in his eyes that he is scared to death. I tell him to put his hands on the truck and not to move. I lower my weapon and ask, "Why were you following me?"

"Someone paid me to follow you."

"Who paid you?"

With desperation in his voice, he answers, "I don't know. The call came through as unknown."

"So how do you contact him?"

"I don't, he calls me."

Before I can ask my next question, I hear sirens. I motion to my stalker to get in the truck. "Tell your friend I'm looking for him and I will find him. Now get out of here."

I figure this person knows nothing. He's just a pawn on the game board. I put my gun away and walk up to the shelter house while repeating aloud the license tag number. I sit down on a picnic table and write the number on the back of one of my business cards. Within seconds, a squad car and an unmarked car pull into the parking lot. I wave.

Big Steve removes his large body from the unmarked car, motions to the two officers in the squad car to stay put, and walks up and takes a seat beside me. "Mickke D, we had a call that someone was pointing a gun at someone in a silver Ford pick-up truck. Do you know anything about that?"

"Yes, detective, that would be me."

"So now you're not only being a pain in the ass, but you're also pointing guns at civilians?"

I cautiously smile. "Well, yes and no. I'm not a pain in the ass, and yes, I was pointing a gun at some low-life, not sure I would even classify him as a civilian."

Steve looks me directly in the eyes and does not smile. "So, where is the gun, and do you have a permit to carry it?"

I hold up my left hand and with my right hand, I slowly retrieve my chrome-plated .45 from its holstered location in the small of my back. I hand it butt first to big Steve. I then get my carry permit from my wallet and hand it to him.

He smells the muzzle and quips, "Well, at least you didn't shoot the guy. Nice .45. Where did you get it?"

"Out of the country while I was in Special Forces. It was a gift from a Colombian general for services rendered."

"I'm not even going to ask what services you rendered to a Colombian general."

It's time to mess with him a bit. "Good, because it's classified, and I couldn't tell you anyway."

He just shakes his head. I know he is eating this to and fro banter up, "Your permit looks valid. Did you check to see if a South Carolina permit is valid in Ohio?"

"Yes, I did, detective, and it is."

He hands the gun back to me, and asks, "So now for the big question. Why were you pointing a gun at this so-called low-life?"

"Can I answer that off the record?" I am trying not to smile.

He raises his voice. "No, it's not off the record. Why were you pointing a gun at that person? Tell me right now or we can discuss it at the station."

"Okay, don't panic." I tell him how the pick-up had been following me since I left Shaw's and how I lured him here to the shelter house. I tell him I let him go because I figure he is only a pawn, and that he may lead us to whoever hired him.

Again, he raises his voice, "What's that, lead *us* to whoever hired him? Do you even know who this guy is?"

"No I don't, but I did write down his license plate number. Maybe you can run the plate for me," and before he can scold me again, I continue. "And doesn't it seem strange that someone is following me ever since I started looking into Sissy's death and David's death? Maybe neither one of their deaths was an accident."

He stands up, gives me a look of disdain, and says, "Oh, give me the damn plate number and stop pointing guns at civilians."

As he turns and walks away, I call out, "Be sure and tell Sharon I said hello." Just as before, he raises his hand and doesn't answer or look back. I think he is actually enjoying having me back in town. Or not.

❧❦

Detective Reynolds has a big smile on his face as he walks away, but he is not going to let Mickke D know that. He had a hunch that Sissy's death was not an accident and now he has a hunch that maybe David's was not an accident as well. Mickee D can snoop around in ways he can't. He just hopes his old friend isn't killed along the way.

Dale DuPont finally makes it to his house in Basil, which is about ten miles east of Pickerington. He is shaking like a leaf in a windstorm. He has been hooked on pain pills for almost three years after a major back injury and he was promised some freebies if he would just follow some guy around and report back when called. He messed up. The guy spotted him, confronted him, and he thought he was going to die. He has no idea what he will tell his caller. Should he tell him what the guy said or just lie and say he lost him? He takes two more pain pills.

Chapter 9: The Mall

I finally get to the River Valley Mall around 11:00. I go directly to Dick's and ask the first employee I see if Terri Gandy is working today. The employee's name is Sara and she is a lovely thirty-something black woman with a beautiful smile. She tells me Terri is in the shoe department and she gives me a big smile and directions. As I turn and walk away, she calls out, "If she can't help you, come back and maybe I can." I start to turn and say something but decide to continue with the mission.

I reach the shoe department and look around. I notice an employee talking to a younger woman who looks familiar to me. After a few seconds, I remember. I walk up to them and say to the young girl, "So how much money did you take from those old guys on Saturday?"

Both women turn and stare at me with bewilderment in their eyes. The young woman finally beams a huge smile and replies, "Grandpa and I took them for about fifty bucks. Didn't I see you in Root's Saturday morning?"

Terri Gandy interjects, "Samantha, were you and grandpa hustling at Valley View again?"

"No, mom, they made the bet, we just agreed and took them to the cleaners."

Terri frowns, looks at me, and asks, "My daughter the golf pro, and who might you be?"

I get out my business card and hand it to her. "I'm Mickke MacCandlish and I'm a private investigator looking into an accident which took place about five years ago on Allen Road. I understand you were the only witness."

She gazes at the card. "So you're from North Myrtle Beach. What are you doing way up here, and why are you investigating something that was declared an accident five years ago?"

Before I have a chance to answer, she continues, "My husband and I have discussed moving to the Myrtle Beach area. Do you like living there? How are the winters down there?"

I get out my wallet and hand her my real estate card. "I am also a real estate broker in the Myrtle Beach area. I'll be happy to show you and your husband around sometime. To answer your first question, I'm originally from Lancaster and a friend of mine asked me to look into his sister's death. She fell off Mt. Pleasant a couple of weeks ago and died. Her husband was the man killed in the accident on Allen Road. Do you mind if I ask you some questions?"

Terri is speechless. After a few seconds, she answers, "Sure, what would you like to know?"

"How good a look did you get of the vehicle that passed you on the road that night?"

"Well, I don't know. I was talking to Samantha on the phone, and it was dark outside and raining. The black limo was moving rather quickly so I slowed down and pulled off to the edge of the road. I just got a glance as it flashed by."

I decide to plant some doubt in her mind. "And are you sure it was a black limo and not a large black SUV?"

"Well, you know, now that I think about it, maybe it could have been a black SUV. I'm not sure. Does that make a difference?"

"Let me ask you this, when was the last time you saw a large black limo?"

She laughs. "Probably the last time we were in Myrtle Beach."

"And when was the last time you saw a large black SUV?"

"Well, I see them every day!" she exclaims.

Samantha interrupts. "Mom, we were talking about Myrtle Beach and the time you got up on the Queen's Float and did the wave thing. Then you said you had to hang up and call 911, that there had been an accident."

Terri puts her hand up to her mouth. "Oh, my God, it could have been a large black SUV."

"Let me ask you this Terri. Have you ever seen a black SUV on Allen Road before?"

She thinks for a minute. "Sure, several times. Why do you ask?"

"Just gathering information." I thank Terri and ask her if I could call her if I have any further questions. She agrees and gives me her cell phone number. I turn to leave, but before I do, I say to both of them, "I would really appreciate it if you didn't say anything to anybody about our discussion here today."

"Of course, no problem. Good luck with your investigation," Terri replies and Samantha waves and nods her head in agreement.

Chapter 10: First Clues

Around 2:00 in the afternoon, Donna calls Mickke D. "I was right about the information on the stories Sissy was working on at the paper. I found some scribbled notes on her desk calendar. She was working on a story about oil and gas fracking in Fairfield County and she was investigating the possible closing or selling of Anchor Hocking's Distribution Center. She was also looking into the addiction to pain pills, which has surfaced lately as an issue in this area."

He thinks for a minute. "Is there any way you can get me her notes on those stories?"

"Well, I'm sitting at her desk right now. Let me look around and I'll call you back." She carefully and quietly opens all of Sissy's desk drawers; however, she doesn't find anything that resembles notes on any of those cases. As she is fumbling around, she accidently spills a box of paper clips. In the bottom of the small box, she notices a thumb drive which to her seems an odd place to keep one. She looks around, and since no one is paying much attention to what she is doing, she slips the thumb drive in her pocket.

As she is leaving the office, she passes an assistant editor who was working with Sissy and she asks, "Say Kevin, what happened to Sissy's computer? I was going to see if I could piece together some of her stories for you?"

He pauses and then shrugs. "I'm not sure; some security person came by with a letter and took it away."

"What type of security person?"

With a sarcastic look on his face, he answers, "I don't know, he had a badge, and a letter signed by some judge."

"Did you get a name?"

"No, it didn't seem that important at the time. It was the day after they found Sissy's body."

"Did they ever bring the computer back?"

As he is walking away, he responds, "I have no idea."

ॐ◌ॐ

Kevin made up the story about a security person picking up Sissy's computer. As soon as Donna leaves the building, he gets on his cell phone and calls a cell phone number that no one ever answers. He leaves a message knowing someone eventually will call him back from an unknown number. He gets his call back in about five minutes. He tells the caller that someone is trying to find out what happened to Sissy's computer. The caller wants to know who was asking questions. Kevin replies, "Donna Crist."

Kevin, an addict, was told by the unknown caller on the day Sissy was found dead to gather up Sissy's computer and deliver it to a small county park between Pickerington and Canal Winchester. There was a bag with a container of pills waiting for him. He had driven to the park, picked up the bag, and left the computer without thinking twice. Now, Kevin wishes he had never said anything to Donna. He should have just said he had no idea where her computer was. Now if she goes to the boss and starts asking questions, he is going to be in hot water.

ॐ◌ॐ

Kevin's caller now has three situations to deal with. Kevin is getting jumpy, and anytime you deal with an addict you are dealing with uncertainty. The second problem is Donna Crist. Why is she so interested in Sissy's computer? Does it have anything to do with the third problem, the PI in town who is also asking questions?

ॐ◌ॐ

Donna leaves the paper and once she gets in her car, calls Mickke D. "It's Dee Dee, I just found a thumb drive in the bottom of a paper clip box in Sissy's desk. I'm going to plug it in to see what's on it."

He quickly replies, "No, someone could be watching you. Meet me in the bar at Shaw's and bring the thumb drive. I'll be at the same table and I'll bring my laptop."

"Okay, and by the way. Someone came into the paper on Tuesday, the day after they found Sissy's body, and took her computer. One of Sissy's assistant editors told me he had a badge, and a paper signed by some judge."

"And no one questioned that at the paper?"

"Well, I guess not. Do you want me to ask around and see what I can find out?"

"No, not right now. Just come on over to Shaw's."

Chapter 11: The Thumb Drive

Before I go down to the bar to meet Donna, I call big Steve. I need him to look into something else for me. "Hey detective, I need another favor." Before he can say no, I continue, "Could you check to see if any other crimes have been committed where a cell phone was not found and maybe go back at least five years?"

Again, the dropped call syndrome. Finally, he replies, "So I guess you want me to go back to around the time of David's accident?"

"Well, the time period has to begin and end sometime. That date is as good as any other. Oh, and by the way, did you find out who was driving the pick-up truck this morning?"

He actually sounds calm to me. "Yes, I did. His name is Dale DuPont. He's 39 and he lives in Basil. He is a divorced engineering consultant with no record, not even a parking ticket."

"That's strange; he seemed to be high on something. I thought for sure he would have a drug arrest record. So, do you have an address for him?" I pleadingly ask.

"And if I give it to you, are you going to bang on his door in the middle of the night and stick your gun up his nose until he breaks down and tells you who hired him?"

"That's a good idea Steve, I hadn't thought about that. Do you think it would work?" After a pause and no answer from him, I continue, "You know I can go on the internet and find his address."

Big Steve gives me Dale's address and tells me not to do anything stupid. He reminds me that if Dale is a druggie, he will shoot first and ask questions later. And since I wasn't a cop, he could claim I was trying to break into his home. Just as I am about to hang up, I ask one more question, "By the way, have you found anyone at Standing Oaks Estates who owns a black Chevy SUV?"

"Haven't got that info yet. Should I bill you by the hour or on a per diem basis?"

"I'll tell you what I'll do. I'll take you and Sharon out to dinner some night. How would that be?"

He replies, "I'll let you know," and hangs up.

I leave my room and venture down to the lobby of Shaw's with my laptop strapped over my shoulder and secured in my Lands End Carry-All. I have my .45 stuck in one of the inside pockets of the bag. The end with my gun is not zipped shut, so I can quickly get to it. Instead of going immediately into the bar area, I go out the side door and take a slow walk around the outside of the building. I'm looking for anything or anyone that looks out of place. I don't notice anything or anyone, which puts me in a quandary.

As I venture into the bar area, there's a show-card stating that The American Songbook Trio will be appearing tonight. Sounds like fun. I may have to come back for that. I go inside and just as I take a seat at the table, Donna walks in. She sits down and hands me the thumb drive.

I look around for Michelle, but she is nowhere to be found. A different but very attractive waitress with dark hair and a sexy short, black skirt shows up and says her name is Tina. I ask if Michelle is working and she says no, today is her day off. We both order a Diet Coke and as I watch Tina walk away, Donna remarks, "Do you know her also?"

I ignore her comment, boot up my laptop, and put in the thumb drive. Several pages of notes appear on my screen. She mentions names, dates, phone numbers, and what transpired at the meetings. Her notes are very concise and easy to read. I look at Donna and ask, "Do you mind if I keep this for awhile?"

"Of course not, I doubt if anyone knows that it exists and no one saw me take it."

"Well, whatever you do, don't mention the fact that it does exist to anyone, and don't ask anyone about Sissy's computer. And, by the way, who is the guy in charge at the paper? I would like to speak with him."

In a rather defiant tone of voice, she replies, "The *woman* in charge is Cathy S. Central. I'll be happy to set up a meeting for you, and don't worry, my lips are sealed."

Sheepishly, I reply, "Sorry, just took for granted it was a man. Yes, please set up a meeting as soon as possible. Thank you."

I walk Donna out to her car and return to my room. Once I get there, I start making notes from Sissy's notes. She has provided me with a list of several people to contact tomorrow. Just as I am almost finished with my note taking, my phone rings. It's big Steve. "I just got the info about black SUVs at Standing Oaks Estates. There are five vehicles matching that description registered with people who live there. Do you want their names? And of course, this information did not come from me."

"Yes, I do, and I will not reveal my sources to anyone. Give them to me." I write down the names and then ask, "By the way, detective, did you ever find Sissy's computer?"

Silence for several seconds. "Why would I be looking for her computer? Remember, this was an accident, not a murder investigation."

"Just covering all bases." I would love to ask about the missing cell phone but I don't want to press my luck. "Thank you, detective. Be sure and let me know about dinner."

He hangs up without answering. I quickly grab my notes from Sissy's thumb drive to see if any of the names match up with the names big Steve just gave me.

Chapter 12: Cathy S. Central

Donna calls me at 8:30 the next morning. "You have an appointment with Cathy at 10:00 this morning. Will that work for you?"

"That's great, Dee Dee. Thank you, I'll be there."

I arrive at The Falcon Express around 9:45 and Cathy comes out to meet me about five minutes later. She is a strikingly attractive woman, I'm guessing in her mid-forties with short blond hair and sporting a very professional dark pants suit. "You must be Mickke D. Donna said you wanted to talk to me about Sissy's death?"

"Yes. Her brother Jake thinks it was a murder and that's why he called me. Do you mind answering a few questions?"

"Not at all, but all I know is what we reported in the paper."

"Let me ask you this. Did Sissy ever get any death threats or harassing phone calls about any of her stories?"

"Death threats, I don't think so, but every good reporter gets those harassing phone calls. You should hear some of the ones I get."

"Did she take any of them seriously?"

"Not that I know of. She never came to me with any complaints."

"What about her husband's death? Was she still investigating that?"

She hesitates for a few seconds and then replies, "That was a tragedy. I don't think she ever got over David's death. She always believed that there was more to the accident than what was reported. Why did you bring up David's accident?"

"No reason." I quickly change the subject. "Do you know who came and got Sissy's computer the day after she was found dead?"

"I have no idea what you're talking about. She usually takes it home with her over the weekend. Who told you someone took it?"

"Donna said she thought it was missing. Maybe it's at her condo."

I thank Cathy and ask her if it's okay to call her if I have any more questions. She gives me her business card and tells me to call anytime.

෴

As soon as I get to my vehicle, I call big Steve. "Did your people ever search Sissy's condo?"

"Not really, we looked around and discovered she was not there and that was about it. Why do you ask?"

"Well, it seems as if her computer is missing. Was it at the condo?"

"I don't remember seeing it, but that doesn't mean it wasn't there. Why are you looking for her computer?"

"Well, if her cell phone is missing and her computer is missing, both of which contain her personal information, that to me would raise a huge red flag. Somebody doesn't want certain information on those devices made public."

"Okay, I'll send some uniforms over there to take a look around."

"Thanks Steve. Call me when they're finished."

෴

I think it's time to have a chat with the person who told Donna that someone picked up Sissy's computer the day after they discovered her body. I call and ask her for a description and the name of the assistant editor. I also ask her if she knows what time he normally goes to lunch.

I park on Chestnut Street just down from the newspaper and wait. At about 12:05, Kevin walks out of the front entrance. I watch him approach in my side view mirror and get out just as he nears the rear of my vehicle.

"Hey, Kevin, do you mind if I ask you some questions? I'm investigating the death of Sissy Adams."

I could see a funny look and irritation in his eyes. His brain was trying to come up with an answer, but the thoughts could not reach his vocal cords. He was at a loss for an answer. Finally, he replies, "Why do you want to talk to me? Are you with the police?"

"No, I'm a private investigator hired to find out what really happened to her." I pull out my wallet, flash my PI ID card, and reach into my shirt pocket and hand him a business card.

He reluctantly accepts my card, looks at it, and then at me. "Sorry, Mr. MacCandlish, I don't know anything except what we print in the paper." He starts to walk away.

I block his path and say, "What about the guy who came and got her computer the day after she was found dead? Did you know him? Can you describe him? Did he show you any ID?"

He hurriedly answers, "He showed me what looked like an official letter and I gave it to him. Now you'll have to excuse me, I'm meeting someone for lunch."

He brushes past me. I let him go but call out, "Thanks Kevin, I'll talk to you later when you have more time."

Chapter 13: Robert Dane

Robert Dane's name was on Sissy's list as a contact person with Wilmont Oil & Gas Company, located in Columbus. He is the vice president in charge of leasing and acquisitions with the company. His job is to oversee all of the company's landmen, the people who go out and acquire oil and gas leases from the landowners and all rights of way and other acquisitions necessary to complete the drilling of a well and putting it on line. He also serves as the public relations contact for the company.

Robert's secretary Marian knocks and then opens his office door and goes in, closing the door behind her. "There is a Mr. MacCandlish here and he would like to speak with you." She hands a business card to him. "I told him you had a busy schedule and that he should make an appointment." Robert gazes at the card, hesitates, and then motions for Marian to show him in.

He greets his guest at the door, shakes his hand, and says, "Sit down, Mr. MacCandlish. I don't get many visits from private investigators. Your card says you are from North Myrtle Beach. I've played a lot of golf down there, or at least I used to before the drilling boom started again. Now I hardly have time to play here. What can I help you with?"

His guest replies, "Thanks for seeing me, Mr. Dane. I'm investigating the death of a newspaper reporter in Lancaster. You may have seen the story in the paper. Her name was Sissy Adams. She fell off of Mt. Pleasant and was killed."

His face shows honest concern. "No, I didn't. Oh my goodness, I did a phone interview with her when we first began drilling in Fairfield County. What a shame."

"Yes, it was. Her brother hired me to look into her death. He thinks she was murdered."

He listens for any change in Mr. Dane's voice or any looks of nervousness on his part after he throws out the word *murder.* He sees no change. He is very calm and collected. "And what does any of this have to do with me, Mr. MacCandlish?"

"Oh, probably nothing, Mr. Dane, I'm just following up with all of the people who Sissy was doing a story on. What was Sissy discussing with you?"

"Well, she was concerned about fracking and that the process would contaminate the underground aquifer which Lancaster and the county utilize for drinking water or that contaminated water would leak from the holding ponds before it was picked up and processed. I assured her that the odds of that happening were astronomical."

"And what would happen if that aquifer became contaminated from fracking?"

"If that happened, our operations would be shut down, so we are very careful to make sure that doesn't happen. We hire a company to test the water to make sure it is clear of any chemicals that might be attributed to us."

With a quizzical look on his face, Mickke D ask, "Pardon my stupidity, but what exactly is fracking?"

"Well, it's actually hydraulic fracturing. It's when they pump huge amounts of high pressure water and chemicals, as well as large amounts of special sand, underground to break shale rock and release the oil and natural gas inside. The sand is used to prop open the paper-thin cracks fracking makes in the shale."

"So is the sand you use like beach sand?"

"No, it's a specific type of sand. It's not what you would find on the beach. We use rounded quartz sand because it's strong enough to handle the pressure and depth involved in fracking. Beach sand is too angular and full of impurities."

Mickke D decides it's time for a zinger. "Did you know that according to Sissy's notes, she was considering hiring an attorney to file an injunction against fracking in Fairfield County until further tests and studies by independent companies could be completed?"

He notices a sudden change in Mr. Dane's demeanor. He can tell he is starting to get irritated. Mr. Dane stands up and says, "I'm sorry to hear about Miss Adams, but I have a lot of things on my plate right now, Mr. MacCandlish. If I can be of any further assistance to you, give my secretary a call and she'll set up an appointment. Nice meeting you Mr. MacCandlish." He ushers him out the door. Mickke D presumes the word *injunction* hit a nerve with him.

As he leaves, he throws out another little jab. "Mr. Dane, you look familiar to me. Did I see you out on Allen Road last Saturday in a black SUV?"

"It's possible, I live just outside of Pickerington but I don't think I was on Allen Road last Saturday. Nice meeting you Mr. MacCandlish." Without offering to shake his hand, he returns to his office, closing the door on his way through.

Marian gives him an adoring smile and says, "Leave me one of your cards, Mr. MacCandlish, so I'll have it when you hopefully call again."

He does as she asks and she hands him one of hers as well. As he takes the card, he clasps her hand. "Thank you Marian, I may call sooner than you think."

She winks, "Promises, promises."

He's thinking this woman could be an excellent contact into the inner sanctum of Wilmont Oil & Gas. She's also very good-looking.

Robert Dane waits a few minutes and then buzzes his secretary. "Marian, get Mr. Peterson on the phone and ask him to call me on my cell phone."

Five minutes later, his cell phone rings. "Robert, its Stu. What's up?"

"I need you to run a background check on a guy. His name is Mickke MacCandlish and he's from North Myrtle Beach, SC. He's a private investigator. Call me as soon as you get the info. Thanks, Stu."

"No problem, Robert. I should know something by this afternoon."

≈≫≪

Stuart Peterson, aka Stu, is a private security contractor. He is 38 years old and an ex-CIA agent with a degree in computer science and analysis. He will work for whoever pays him and his fees are not cheap. He works on a per diem basis and charges $350 a day plus expenses, and if he only works one hour that is the same as a half day to him. He lets his clients know that if there is any information on the internet, he will find the person they are looking for and eliminate them if need be. He can't think of anything he wouldn't do if paid enough by a client. His clients know he may be working for other clients but they never know whom and they know better than to ask. He is very private, tight-lipped, and without morals or fear. He is currently under contract to three different clients in the central Ohio area, and one of those is Wilmont Oil & Gas.

≈≫≪

Around 1:00 that afternoon, Robert's phone rings and Stu's phone number pops up. "Hey, Stu. What did you find out?"

"Well, he's originally from Lancaster, 45 years old, and ex-Special Forces. He is the broker in charge of his own real estate company, Mickke D Realty, and runs a private investigation company, Grand Strand Investigations. Seems as though he is well off financially and has been involved with several investigations in the Myrtle Beach area. He's currently not married, although he has been divorced three times. In his spare time, he helps on ocean salvage jobs in the area. It seems as if he has his shit together except for the ex-wife thing."

Robert makes some notes and then replies, "Thanks. I'll let you know if I need anything else."

The next call Robert makes is to his boss. "I had a meeting with a private investigator from South Carolina earlier today. Said he was investigating the death of Sissy Adams, a reporter down in Lancaster. He also said she was considering an injunction against fracking in Fairfield County at the time of her death."

"So, what's the big deal? The reporter is dead and I haven't received any injunctions to stop fracking. But I wonder how that PI found out about the injunction?"

"You sound as if you knew she was dead?"

"Sure I knew. I read it in the paper. You didn't know?"

"No, I must have missed it. It would have been nice if someone had let me know. That way that PI today wouldn't have blindsided me. So what do you want me to do? I already had Stu do a background check on the guy." Robert relays the information Stu had given him on Mr. MacCandlish.

"Sounds like quite an adversary, Robert. I would still like to know where he got that Information."

"Well, I suppose we could have Stu have an up-close and personal talk with him."

"Not yet. Let's see what happens, if you hear back from your PI friend, let me know."

Chapter 14: Ginny Ridlinger

After lunch, my next stop is Anchor Hocking Glass. Sissy had spoken to a Ginny Ridlinger, the director of public relations for the company. She was investigating the possible sale of Anchor Hocking and the plant shutting down. That would put a whole lot of people out of work in Lancaster and the surrounding area. Ginny had assured her that no such thing was going to happen.

Anchor Hocking is the second largest employer in Fairfield County. Only the Medical Center and Hospital employs more people. Since I grew up in Lancaster, just the thought of the plant closing down gives me cold chills.

Anchor Hocking Glass began in 1905. The name came from the Hocking River near where the plant was located. In its first year of production, the company made and sold more than $20,000 worth of glassware. That would be equal to about $1.8 million in today's dollars. The development of a revolutionary machine that pressed glass saved the company when the Great Depression hit. The new machine raised production rates from one item per minute to more than thirty items per minute. When the 1929 stock market crash hit, the company responded by developing a fifteen-mold machine that could produce ninety pieces of glass per minute. This allowed the company to survive the depression when so many other companies vanished. Several companies bought and sold the plant since then, but I don't think anyone in Lancaster could ever conceive there not being an Anchor Hocking Plant in town. The effects of that would be devastating to the entire area.

I stop by Anchor's main office at the Distribution Center on West Fair Avenue about 2:00. As I'm walking through the parking lot, I notice a black SUV in a reserved parking space with a GR1U-SAF license tag.

My non-appointment stop to see Mr. Dane earlier that same day had worked so I decided to try the same thing with Ginny Ridlinger. My luck is still holding. Her secretary takes my card and disappears. Shortly thereafter, Ginny comes out to the waiting room. She is an alluring, almost desirable, looking woman; I'm going to guess in her mid-forties. "Mr. MacCandlish, why in the world would a private investigator want to see me? Are you looking for a job?"

My first thought is that this woman had to have been in the military. I'm going to guess Air Force because of the license plate I saw in the parking lot. She just had that "air" about her. She was in charge. I notice a missing wedding ring on her finger and reply, "Excuse me, Ms. Ridlinger, did you ever spend time in the military?"

"Actually I did, but that's none of your business," Her scornful frown changes to an insincere smile. "Now if you would like to set up an appointment, maybe we can work you in later."

I need to change the way this encounter is heading. "Sorry, I spent some time in the military myself and I meant that question only in a respectful way."

She quickly asks, "What branch were you in, Mr. MacCandlish?"

"Army Special Forces, what about you?"

"Twenty years Air Force."

I smile as I catch her glancing at my ring finger, which is also bare. "I'll just bet you were a pilot."

"No, Mr. MacCandlish, I was a surgery technician. I was a body mechanic. And what did you do?"

"Please, call me Mickke D. I used to chase bad guys around."

Her demeanor completely changed. "And what did you do once you caught them?"

"It depended on how bad they were. But hey, I just wanted to ask you a few questions about a case I'm working on."

Her contempt toward me changes. "Come into my office, I have a few minutes to spare." She motions towards a chair. "Sit down, Mr. MacCandlish. Would you care for coffee or something else to drink?"

"No thanks, I'm fine."

The same woman who just minutes ago was going to rip my head off is now becoming very friendly, almost too friendly. The time has come to see what is going on with this woman.

"So what case are you working on Mr. MacCandlish. How can I help?"

"I'm looking into the death of Sissy Adams, the reporter who fell off of Mt. Pleasant a couple of weeks back. Did you know her?"

She responds as if she is carefully choosing her words. "I didn't know her personally, but she did call me about some rumors going around town that the plant was going to be sold and shut down."

"And how did you respond?"

"I told her I had no knowledge of that, which I don't." She gives me a measured stare and then continues, "I'm having a hard time figuring out what her tragic death has to do with me."

"Well, her brother, who is an old friend of mine from high school, thinks she was murdered because of some story she may have been working on for the paper. She mentioned you and Anchor Hocking in her notes. I'm just following up with everyone she had been talking with."

"I can assure you Mr. MacCandlish, I know nothing about that reporter's death except what I read in the paper, and I thought the paper said it had been an accident."

It's time to stir the pot a little bit, "Yes, they did, but there are usually two sides to every story. By the way, you look familiar. Did I see you out on Allen Road this past Saturday driving a black SUV?"

She crosses her arms over her chest, leans back in her chair, and replies, "I don't think so." Then, while staring at the ceiling, she continues, "Let's see, I was in Toledo Saturday at a conference. Any more questions, Mr. MacCandlish?"

"No, I don't think so. Thanks for your help. Oh, by the way, how long have you been with Anchor?

"About two years now. Anything else? Should I call my attorney?"

Well, I don't think so Ms. Ridlinger, however, if I have any further questions, may I call you?"

"Of course you may, here's my personal cell phone number." She writes her number on one of her business cards and escorts me out to the waiting room. "Have a nice day, Mr. MacCandlish."

By the time I get to my vehicle, I am convinced she knows more than what she told me. She was hiding something. I asked her to call me Mickke D and she never did, and she never came back with, "You can call me Ginny." That to me is a sign that I would probably not be on her Christmas card list and that she does not trust me. She said she had been with Anchor about two years, which would have been about the same time the fracking issue came about. Maybe just a coincidence. As soon as I get back to Shaw's, I call Jim and ask him to see what he can find out about Mr. Dane and Ms. Ridlinger.

≈∽

Ginny had been warned to expect a call and minutes after Mickke D leaves her office, she closes her door and places a call on her cell phone. "Well, your PI just left. It seems as if that reporter's brother thinks she was murdered and that's why he is investigating. I don't think he knows anything. He did refer to her notes several times, but he did not specify where he got them and I didn't think I should have asked him where he got them. He did ask me if I was in a black SUV on Allen Road this past Saturday, but of course I told him I was in Toledo."

"Thank you. Call me if he contacts you again."

As soon as the caller hangs up with Ginny, he calls Robert Dane. "Did the PI ask you if you were on Allen Road Saturday?"

"Well, as a matter of fact he did. Does that mean anything?"

"No, I just wanted to know."

Chapter 15: The Winery

I call Jake to see if he wants to go to dinner tonight. He suggests we go up to The Buckeye Lake Winery located on the Thornville side of the lake. He says he will pick me up at 6:00. On the way to dinner, I fill Jake in on my progress since I last spoke with him. I make sure I tell him about what Steve said about decking the next one of us who calls him big Steve. He just laughs.

The winery and restaurant are new to me but I like the atmosphere as soon as we get there. It is comfortable with outdoor seating and has a good feel to it. We order a bottle of wine and dinner. Jake wants to know if there is anything he can do to help, and I just tell him if I need anything I will let him know.

About halfway through dinner, he asks, "So Mickke D, how is your love life these days?"

"Not that great, Jake. I was having a great relationship with a beautiful blond back in Myrtle Beach, and then one day she just disappeared."

"What do you mean, disappeared?"

"Well, one day she was there and the next day her condo was empty and she was nowhere to be found. Let's change the subject." We go back to talking about Sissy.

Just as we are finishing our meal, I get the strange feeling that someone is watching us and that danger is lurking. There is a fairly large crowd on the outside patio area but no one really gets my attention, although there is a table of four very attractive women not far from us who look over every once in a while and smile. I almost say something to Jake, but I keep telling myself I'm here on business not pleasure. Of course, I remember the day when that didn't make a difference. I suppose that's why I've been married, divorced, and broke three times. I guess I'm getting smarter in my old age.

Jake notices the lovely ladies as well and says, "Well, Mickke D, what do you think, should we venture over there and say hello? Maybe we'll get lucky."

"Help yourself Jake, I think I am just going to take a walk around and watch the sunset." I still have that "being watched, danger lurking" feeling in my mind.

"Wait a minute. Who are you and what have you done with my friend Mickke D, the skirt chaser?"

I barely hear his well-meaning but never-the-less shallow analysis because I have just figured out the source of my concern. I notice what looks like a 26-foot antique mahogany four-seat, Criss-Craft speedboat anchored in the lake just off shore. I remember hearing it and then watching it pull in, and it has been there since right after we got here. I have not seen anyone leave the boat. Now why would you bring your boat up to this lovely restaurant and just sit there and not come in for a drink or dinner?

"You know what Jake, why don't you go over to those lovely ladies and see if one of them would come over and take a photo of us, you know, for old time's sake."

However, before he can get up, my wish comes true.

Chapter 16: Stephanie

T.C. has just left My Sister's Books in Pawleys Island, South Carolina. He was returning some old maps that he and Mickke D had borrowed from Susan, one of Bess's customers, and a close friend of Mickke D's. They had been going over the maps to see if they could figure out where some buried treasure might possibly be located. He is on his way to the Georgetown Library to look at some more maps that he hopes may help. As he passes The Hammock Shops, he glances over and sees a woman getting into her car. "Oh my God, it can't be," he half whispers to himself.

The woman he just saw almost reminds him of Stephanie Langchester, a marine biologist from England who was helping him with a salvage operation off the coast of Pawleys Island. She and three other girls had stolen his 46-foot Carver and most of the artifacts found on *The Queen Beth*, a wrecked pirate ship from circa 1700. He has not seen or heard from any of them since the robbery. He did get his boat back but none of the artifacts. As far as he knows, the authorities were unable to locate any of the girls.

He pulls off the highway and watches as the car with the Stephanie look-alike leaves The Hammock Shops and goes north toward Litchfield. The only reason he noticed her was that the woman was noticeably tall and had the same type of walk. Stephanie was tall but she had short hair. This woman had long hair and glasses. The only glasses he ever saw on Stephanie were sunglasses. He thinks about following her but decides it is just a moment in time and proceeds south to Georgetown.

❧❦

Stephanie Langchester is indeed back in town. She has been living in a beautiful rented apartment under an assumed name on Antigua in the Caribbean. Stephanie is a marine biologist and former agent with British Intelligence. She and the other three girls had come to Myrtle Beach to help with the salvage operation on *The Queen Beth*. It had been her plan to steal all of the artifacts, gold, silver, and jewels from the operation, split the money, and live happily ever after. Well, that didn't work out. She discovered that the gold, silver, and jewels had been moved on shore and buried. She even has what she thinks is a map showing where the treasure resides. The problem is the crude map would have been drawn back in the early 1700s and the coastline has changed since then. She and the girls took what they could, split up, though not on good terms, and left the country.

She knows her height is a dead giveaway so she wore flat shoes and a wig and made herself look like an old lady leaning over a cane to get back into the country. She came by boat because there were fewer security checks. Once in the U.S., she changed wigs and got rid of the cane. The only people who could possibly recognize her are TC or Mickke D. However, what are the odds of running into them?

Recently, through her old intelligence network, she had discovered the other three girls had been killed and everyone thinks she did it. British Intelligence has put a large price on her head. She may have cheated the other girls out of some money, but she did not kill them, and now she is trying to figure out who did.

Still, she has been unable to get the buried treasure out of her mind. She figures it has to be worth tens of millions. Hence the trip back to Myrtle Beach. While doing some research on the internet, she found a reference to some old maps at the Georgetown Library. Her plan is to check out those maps before going to Charleston to do a little snooping around and then back to Antigua. She learned in the intelligence business that the longer you stay in an area, the better the odds are of someone recognizing you.

Chapter: 17 Girls, Boats & Bats

I feel someone approaching. I turn, look up, and there is this beautiful woman looking at me and smiling. She is maybe in her late thirties or early forties with short, dark hair. She is one of the four women I noticed at the other table. "Excuse me, but aren't you Mickke MacCandlish?"

I am completely caught off guard and I just stare at her without speaking. My mind is somewhere else. Finally, Jake breaks the silence, "Yes, he is Mickke MacCandlish, but he's always been rather shy around beautiful women."

"Well, I'm Sherie Small and you used to date my older sister Sandy Derr in high school, but I don't remember her saying anything about you being shy. She used to tell me to stay in my room when you would come over to the house when mom and dad were gone."

I feel my face turning red and my mind is trying to put this whole thing together. Finally, I stand up and say, "Now I remember. Sandy Derr, cute girl with red hair and wore glasses. Of course, you're her younger sister Sherie. How are you, and how is Sandy?"

"She's married to a professional fisherman, lives in Long Boat Key, Florida, and has two kids, but she always had this huge crush on you. I thought that was you and I just wanted to say hello."

I now know what to do. I pull out my cell phone, hand it to Jake, and say, "Jake why don't you take a picture of Sherie and me? And be sure to get that beautiful boat out there in the lake in the picture as well."

Jake has a perplexed look on his face, but he takes the phone as Sherie sits down in the chair next to me. I put my arm around her and smile at Jake. I hear the roar of the large inboard motors from the Criss-Craft come to life. "Any time Jake, while we're all still young."

Jake takes the photo. "Take another one Jake, just in case."

Sherie pulls out her phone and asks Jake to take one with her phone. She wants to send it to Sandy. Jake takes the photo as the boat leaves the area.

I look out toward the lake and the approaching sunset as the antique Criss-Craft boat disappears. Jake and I walk Sherie back to her table and she makes introductions all around. Jake seems disappointed because all four women are all sporting wedding rings.

After some small talk, we return to our table and Jake exclaims, "I don't ever remember you dating Sandy Derr in high school and I don't remember her having a gorgeous younger sister. Where was I?"

I give Jake a stare. "Remember Jake, I wasn't the one to kiss and tell. That was you, not me. There were a lot of girls I dated in high school that you never knew about."

Jake sighs, "Oh well, what a bummer. I guess we won't get lucky tonight. And why did you want that boat in the picture?"

"Just a hunch Jake, just a hunch."

I grab my phone and gaze at the two pictures Jake took. The boat shows up well in both of them. I email both pictures to Steve and text him to see if he can figure out who owns the boat. I may make some stops at a few of the local marinas here on the lake to see if they know who owns the boat.

"All in all Jake, this was a pretty good night. Even though we did not get lucky, I did fine because you drove and you're paying for dinner."

"Right, and are you going to tell me who else you dated that I don't know about?"

"No way Jake, no way."

❧❦

We leave the winery, and just before we get to the paved highway, we encounter a detour sign pointing us down a dirt road. The signs don't appear very official to me but Jake turns before I have a chance to stop him. "Jake, I don't think this is a good idea. Did you see anything wrong on the other road?"

It's too late. A pickup truck pulls out of the woods in front of us and another one pulls in behind us. We have nowhere to go. Two rather burly, menacing-looking figures get out of the front truck and a guy who looks like Paul Bunyan gets out of the truck behind us. All three look like scalawags from the lower end of the food chain.

I immediately say to Jake, "Get out of the car now. We don't need to be stuck in this car. Stand back to back, and if I tell you to run, do it and don't look back."

By this time, Jake's eyes are the size of saucers and getting bigger by the second. It's dusk and getting darker by the minute. "Say what?" he finally blurts out.

"Just do it Jake, now!" I say with a very stern look his way.

The headlights from the opposing trucks are shining right in our eyes. Before I went into the winery, I put my weapon in Jake's glove compartment. I retrieve it before exiting the car and place it in my right front pants pocket. I quickly dial 911 on my phone and place it in my left front pants pocket.

We venture out to the middle of the road and as I told Jake, we stand back to back. I gaze at the two guys in front of me who both have baseball bats. I turn and look over my shoulder and see Paul Bunyan has one as well. I'm beginning to feel better. If they were going to kill us, we would already see weapons. I say to the two in front of me, "Say fellows, what seems to be the problem?"

The biggest one barks back, "The trouble is, asshole, we don't like you. Take your hands out of your pockets."

I try smiling as I reply, "Now how can you not like me? You don't even know me. And if I take my hands out of my pockets, you're really not going to like me." I take my left hand out and show him my phone. "I've already dialed 911, why don't you guys just leave before the police get here."

The big guy lifts his ball bat and comes toward me. I pull my .45 from my other pocket and fire a shot that hits about two feet in front of him. He stops.

Jake calls out, "Mickke D, here comes the other one. Should I run now?"

"No Jake, just duck, now!" Jake ducks and I turn and see Mr. Bunyan coming our way. He is not going to stop. I fire one time and hit him in the shoulder. He stops and falls to his knees. I hear a yell from Jake, turn back the other way and here come the other two. I fire at the closest one and hit him in the kneecap. He goes down. The third one stops and raises his hands.

"Jake, get on your phone and call 911 just in case mine didn't go through." Jake is just staring at the guy who is holding his knee and screaming. "Wake up Jake, make the call."

"You shot them," Jake slowly replies. "You shot them."

"Well, I didn't kill them. Did you want me to wait until they beat us severely about the head and shoulder region, or did you want to be used for batting practice?"

Jake calls 911 and with a shaky voice tells the operator where we are located. I walk over to the third guy and tell him to put his hands on the truck. "Jake, take his belt off and give it to me."

"Why do you want his belt?" Jake is still in a daze.

"Jake, you ask a lot of questions. So I can tie him up. I don't think the other two will be running away."

I search the third guy, tie his hands behind his back, and sit him against the truck. I go to Paul Bunyan and carefully search him as well. He is still emitting an aura of danger and a smell of alcohol. I tell Jake to search both trucks for weapons. Both pickups have a rifle rack over the rear window with a .30-.30 caliber rifle in place. I give one rifle to Jake, make sure it's loaded, and tell him to watch Paul Bunyan. I search the other guy as well and tell him to stop yelling, that they make artificial knees. I tell him I was aiming at his head. He's just lucky I missed.

I go back over to the tied-up guy and ask him why they were going to attack us with ball bats. He says, with alcohol on his breath and without hesitation, that a guy came into the bar just up the road and said he wanted to get a couple of guys' attention. "He gave each of us a hundred-dollar bill. He told us where you were and what you were driving."

"Did you ask him if I was packing?"

He just grunts.

"What did the man look like?" I ask.

"He was, I don't know, maybe about 5'10 or 5'11, maybe 170 pounds, wearing a hoodie. I never really saw his face."

We now hear sirens heading our way, and within minutes two sheriff's cruisers plus an EMS vehicle pull up to our location. They cautiously exit their vehicles and tell us to raise our hands. We both do as they say.

After explaining what happened, they seem to believe us but one of the deputies ask if there is someone who can vouch for us. I give them big Steve's name and number. He makes a call and tells us to follow them to the Sheriff's Office in Lancaster. We agree.

On the way back to town, I drive because Jake is too shook up to talk, let alone drive a car. After both of us give a statement, we finally get to leave around 11:00 but we are told to be available if needed. Jake drives back to Shaw's and drops me off. I ask him, "Would you like to try a different place for dinner tomorrow night?"

He looks at me, turns back, but does not answer. I get out of the car and he drives away. I guess he has never been in a situation such as he encountered tonight.

Stuart Peterson was watching the altercation at Buckeye Lake from a concealed location. Earlier he had given a guy four one hundred-dollar bills, one for him and three to have the job done. He was told to go into the bar and have three heavies have a sincere talk with two guys who were having dinner at The Winery. He passed on a description of the vehicle they were driving. He waited outside the bar to make sure his messenger did what he was supposed to do and not pocket the money and run.

That ploy didn't work, so now it is time to take care of this problem another way. Up to this point, he thought a scare might send this PI packing and on his way back home. Now it is time to get serious. It is time to tie up some loose ends.

≈∞

As Jake leaves and before I go inside, I walk around Shaw's. I see no sign of a black SUV or silver Ford pickup. I look across the street at Fairfield Federal's parking lot, but it is empty. I go in the front door and as I walk into the lobby, I see big Steve sitting in one of the over-sized lounge chairs. He is not smiling. I wave and he just points to the other chair next to his. "Mickke D, you are becoming a bigger pain in the ass every day you're in town. First, you point a gun at a civilian and now you shoot two of them. You are becoming a menace to Lancaster society."

I give him a sullen look. "Well, I didn't kill either one of them. That one lowlife looked like Paul Bunyan, they all had baseball bats, and they were highly intoxicated. What did you want me to do, ask them how their day was going?"

I see the beginnings of a smile on his face but it doesn't last long. "You're lucky Mickke D. That big guy was Billy Barr, a local misfit from the area. He's spent time in every jail in the county. The other big guy was his brother Jason Barr, and the other guy, the only one you didn't shoot, was their cousin, Joey Sheets."

"The guy I didn't shoot told me that a guy came into the bar and offered each of them a hundred-dollar bill to rough us up a little. Is that what he told the deputies?"

This time he does laugh. "No, as a matter of fact, all three of them said you and Jake started a fight and they were just defending themselves. They want you and Jake arrested on assault and battery charges. But each of them did have a hundred-dollar bill in their possession, as well as baseball bats."

I have no comeback. I just shake my head and change the subject. "Did you get the pictures I sent you of the boat at The Winery?"

"I did, but why do you want to know who owns it?"

"Because it pulled in right after we arrived. No one ever left the boat and the inhabitants decided to leave as soon as we started taking pictures. Then Jake and I are attacked after leaving the restaurant. Sounds like a set-up to me."

"Well, if I were you, Mickke D, I would check with some of the marinas in the area to see if any of them know who owns the boat. I can't send more people out on a closed case, and I have no way of figuring out who owns the boat any other way." After a slight pause he continues, "I'll see what I can find out for you."

I give him a hard stare. "Thank you. Any other news for me?"

"Yes. I found a case back around the time of David's death where a cell phone was missing and never found. The victim was the wife of State Representative Michael North. She drowned in a bathtub in a motel from a mixture of pain pills and booze about three weeks after David died. Her cell phone was never recovered."

"That's interesting. One of the stories Sissy was working on had to do with illegal pain pills. Is there any way I can see the file?"

"I'll see what I can do, but the case was filed and closed as an accidental overdose. There were no bruises on the body and she had checked in by herself."

I quickly reply, "Except for the missing cell phone. Just like the fact that Sissy's phone was never found."

"Okay, I told you I will see what I can do." He stands up, turns toward the front entrance, and then turns back and says, "I would suggest you keep your head down. Sounds like someone has it in for you."

I reply sarcastically, "I didn't know you cared."

"I don't, but Sharon said we would love to go to dinner with you and I want to be able to collect on your offer."

I go up to my room, reload my .45, take a hot shower, and fall asleep the second I hit the bed. I'm getting way too old for this line of work.

Chapter 18: The Brothers

Around 10:00, the following morning Jim from Myrtle Beach calls. "How are things in Ohio? Did you get those Buckeye shirts for me?"

"Things are so-so, and no I haven't. Someone tried to get my attention with a baseball bat last night but other than that, not much going on. Did you find out anything for me?"

"Are you okay? You don't sound any worse for wear. Did you deck the guy? "

"No, I shot him and his brother."

After a slight pause, he replies, "Are you sure you don't want me to come up there and lend a hand?"

"No, all is well for now. So what did you find out?"

"Here's what I have. Thought I would tell you and then email you. Are you ready?"

"Yes."

"Well, Robert Dane has no record at all. Been in the oil and gas industry all his life. He has had a few financial problems before the recent boom but seems solvent now. The company he works for, Wilmont Oil & Gas, is not so clean. They have had several environmental fines thrown their way, totaling over five million dollars, as well as some labor disputes. Several lawsuits filed but they usually settle out of court. The president is a Mr. Von Spineback who lives in Bexely, Ohio."

"Wait a minute, did you say Spineback?"

"Yeah, his first name is Von, that's with a `v` like in victory."

"That's interesting, I have a Jon Spineback on my list of people to talk to, but he lives just outside of Pickerington. See if you can find a connection for me."

"You got it. Now as far as Ms. Ridlinger is concerned, be careful. She spent 20 years in the Air Force, black belt, expert marksman, and was reprimanded twice for beating the crap out of a couple of civilians although they started it both times. She's divorced with no kids. Seems to be financially well off with a decent pension and a good job."

"Yeah, when I met her, I could tell she had her shit together. Thanks Jim, this case is starting to get very interesting. I'll talk to you later."

"Hey, don't forget my Ohio State T-Shirts and maybe a sweat-shirt or two."

"No problem big guy, got you covered."

Fifteen minutes later, Jim calls back and reports, "Jon and Von Spineback are twin brothers."

&oc

Jon and Von Spineback are indeed identical twins, but that's where the relationship ends. The boys were always very competitive in school and several times it ended in a knock-down drag-out fight. They got to the point where they just did not like each other. Now the only time they see each other is when their mom forces them to come over for Thanksgiving and Christmas. They usually say hello and goodbye.

Jon went to college and on to medical school while Von rebelled and didn't attend college. He traveled around the country for a while, did a stint in the Air Force, and then took a job as a landman with Wilmont Oil & Gas Company. He was very good at leasing ground for the company and acquiring rights of ways for pipelines. He was quickly promoted to director of gas marketing and supply for the company and then vice president of operations. He was known as a no-nonsense, do anything to get the job done type of person, which did not sit well with some of the other officials in the company. After the president had a sudden heart attack and died, Von was appointed president of Wilmont Oil & Gas by the board of directors. He has been with the company for twenty years.

Chapter 19: Addicted

About 10:30 that same day, Kevin receives a call from his unknown caller friend. "I need you to go to the park between Pickerington and Canal Winchester and pick up a brown paper bag with some pills inside as a thank you for your help with the computer. The pill bag will be in a plastic bag inside the trash can near the entrance to the lake. Thanks again for all of your help."

Kevin is a little suspicious, but any time he can get free pills, he's all in. He has severe headaches and the doctors have no idea what is causing them so they kept prescribing medicine. Now Kevin can't go without them.

He leaves the newspaper at 11:30 and drives up 33 to Allen Road, takes Allen to 256, and slows down as he passes the location where Sissy's husband David was killed. He continues through Pickerington and arrives at the park around 12:10. There are only two other cars in the parking lot, which seems a little strange to him since it is lunch time and quite a few people come here to have lunch and a short walk before returning to the office.

He exits his vehicle and walks toward the trash can, which sits next to the path leading to the small lake. He looks around and sees no one. He takes off the lid and sees the plastic bag, which is tied at the top. He takes out the bag and replaces the lid. He looks around again and still sees no one. He returns to his car and opens the plastic bag. Inside is a small brown paper bag, which is stapled shut. He opens the brown bag and finds a non-labeled bottle of pills. It looks like there could be probably twenty-five or thirty white pills inside. Under the container, he sees a note. He takes the piece of paper out of the bag and reads it. "Thank you. It would be very nice if Donna Crist has an accident. There are more pills where these came from."

Kevin doesn't know what to think. He just sits there and stares out the windshield. Does the guy want him to kill her or just hurt her? He immediately calls the non-answering number and waits, but his call is not returned. He is confused, but he does know one thing for sure. He is not a killer. However, he knows he is addicted to pain pills. He slowly leaves the park and returns to the newspaper without having lunch. He pops a couple of pills instead and notices a strange taste left in his mouth. He figures they are probably okay, or else why would the caller ask him to hurt Donna? The rest of his afternoon is pretty much a blur.

ॐ∽

The anonymous caller hopes that Kevin takes care of Donna Crist in a hurry. The pain pills are coated with brine from the leaves of the rhubarb plant. The stalks of the plant are delicious and make great pies, but the leaves are poisonous and are cut off, left on the soil to decompose and nourish future crops. He is slowly killing himself every time he pops a pill.

Chapter 20: Close Encounter

TC finishes looking over some of the maps at the Georgetown Library without much success. He plans to come back tomorrow morning and start over again. This whole thing with the treasure map and a possible treasure discovery is invigorating to him. He doesn't need the money, but the idea of finding buried treasure from the early 1700s is a driving force. He can't decide whether he wants to continue looking around Georgetown for the treasure or to pursue the possible salvage job in the Caribbean. He will probably wait until Mickke D returns from Ohio to make the final decision. Of course, if he thinks he has discovered the location of the buried treasure, the decision will be easy.

❧☙

Stephanie Langchester arrives at the Georgetown Library as TC exits the building. She spots him immediately and ducks down in the front seat of her rented car. If she had arrived five minutes sooner, she would have passed him on the steps to the library. Would he have recognized her? Maybe, maybe not, but she is very happy the chance meeting did not occur.

She slowly raises her head and peers over the top of the steering wheel as TC saunters by her, not thirty feet away. She watches as he enters his vehicle and slowly leaves the library parking lot. She looks at her watch and waits for ten minutes before exiting her car. She wants to be sure he does not return.

She quickly crosses the lot and proceeds into the library. She goes directly to the front desk and asks in her best Southern drawl. "Are there are any old maps anywhere in the library that may show old coastlines?"

The woman looks at her strangely and says, "That's funny, a man just left not too long ago who was also looking for old coastline maps. We have some old maps from the mid 1600s to the late 1700s back on the far left corner of the library. There is a table there that you may use to look at them."

Stephanie thanks the woman and starts to turn away. She stops and turns back to the woman and sort of whispers, "I'm doing some research for a documentary film company, so I would appreciate it if y'all did not mention my visit to anyone. We're trying to keep it on the quiet side until we're ready to start shooting. Maybe we could find a place for y'all in our film. Do y'all have a card?"

The woman looks pleasantly flustered. "Oh, I won't say a word to anyone. Here's my card. I would be more than happy to appear in your film."

Stephanie gazes at the card. "Thanks Penne, I will keep y'all in mind." She puts her finger to her lips and turns back to continue her research in the rear of the library. She spends about an hour looking over maps before the library closes and does not find anything which might be beneficial of her pursuit of the buried treasure. She will need to come back at another time. Before leaving, she asks Penne, "I will need to return later on, do y'all know if that gentleman who was looking at the same maps will be returning?"

Penne whispers, "Yes, he told me he will be coming back tomorrow morning."

Stephanie thinks for a few seconds and then replies, "Penne, do y'all think if I call ahead of time and ask if he is using the maps, y'all could let me know?"

Again, she whispers, "Oh, no problem. I'll be happy to help you anyway I can."

Stephanie thanks Penne and leaves the library. She is staying in Charleston, which is about an hour away. She needs to make a stop at the marina where she made the deal to sell TC's boat before she calls it a night.

☙❧

She had made the arrangement with some guys at this out-of-the-way marina to purchase TC's boat for $150,000 in cash, no questions asked. The marina is a small, obscure marina on the edge of Mt. Pleasant, which is located just north of Charleston. She had never met the party she spoke with and they did not know her. She wanted to nose around and see if they knew anything about the death of the three girls.

The person she had spoken to and made the deal with was Danny Dykes. He had told her the money would be waiting and as long as the boat was as nice as she had described, there would be no problems. The girls had received their money and the marina provided a rental boat to take them on to Key West.

The problem had occurred several days later when the FBI came to the marina, confiscated the boat, and arrested Danny and his crew. TC had placed a GPS transponder in the boat so it could be traced with a GPS tracking system. He reclaimed the boat, and Danny was out $150,000, which, by the way, he had borrowed from some rather unscrupulous underworld characters with ties to the mob. He had also spent around $7,500 of his own money to repaint the boat, change its appearance, and change the name. His plan had been to sell the boat to a Saudi businessman for $450,000 and pocket a cool $295,000.

In court, Danny and his crew had pleaded ignorance; they had no idea the boat was stolen, and they were let out on bail. Danny and his crew were not happy campers. They went to work trying to find out where the three girls were and to recoup their losses.

Chapter 21: Mt. Pleasant

I've been in Lancaster for four days now and so far, a rent-a-cop stopped me, Dale DuPont stalked me, and three guys with baseball bats attacked me. In addition, I am no closer to figuring out who killed Sissy than I was the day I arrived. I have considered going to Dale DuPont's house in Basil and having an up close and personal talk with him, but I really don't believe he knows much.

Therefore, since it's a beautiful day, I opt to go back up on Mt. Pleasant and do some exploring for a few hours. Maybe the climb will clear my head and give me a new perspective on this case. In addition, maybe, just maybe, someone new will follow me and I'll have a new person of interest to question. I pay close attention on the way over, but do not notice anyone following me.

I guess my jogging and walking around downtown Lancaster has done me some good because it is much easier to get to the top this time, although I do make one rest stop along the way. Once I arrive at the top, there are several families with cameras and other singles just milling about or standing by the railing looking out at the sights. As I approach, no one seems the least bit interested in the fact that I am there and pays no attention to me. No one looks familiar. The hairs on the back of my neck are still where they should be so I decide to go off and explore in another direction.

I start down the path toward Devil's Kitchen, but I notice what looks like a little-used path heading the other direction, away from Devil's Kitchen. It may just be an animal trail of some kind, but what the hell; I slowly begin to follow it. It is not an easy walk and it is about twenty feet below the rim of the mountain on a narrow ledge. After about ten minutes and as I turn a sharp corner, the path suddenly and abruptly ends into a pile of rocks and trees. Now most people would have stopped there and turned around, and maybe I would have in my teenage years, but my Special Forces training kicks in. I remember being told several times that just because the trail ends, doesn't mean it has stopped. We were always taught to look on the other side to see if the trail picks up again. That will not be easy. There is about a 200-foot drop-off to one side and a 20-foot-high wall of rocks and trees on the other side.

There are two trees on this small path blocking my way. Their trunks are growing close together but about ten feet up they split, and it looks to me like enough room for me to squeeze through and get over to the other side.

Just as I am preparing to shimmy up between the two trees, I hear a twig snap. The hair on the back of my neck does its thing, next comes fear, then the brain's will to survive. I guess I should have paid better attention on my drive over here. As I slowly turn around with .45 in hand, I quickly determine that someone did indeed follow me.

Chapter 22: Revenge #1

Stephanie pulls into the marina parking lot, puts on her wig and glasses, and picks up her cane. She slowly meanders into the marina office. A middle-aged man with shorts, a beach shirt, and boat shoes asks if he can help her with anything. "Well, I hope so" she answers. "I saw an ad online not too long ago that said you had a 46-foot Carver for sale. Is it still available?"

He gives her an odd look. "Sorry lady, never had a boat like that here. You might try on down the road in Charleston. I've got a few smaller boats here for sale but nothing that big."

"So does that mean you never had a boat like that or you just don't have one now?" she says with authority in her voice.

"Look lady, I told you I don't have a Carver that size here. Now is there anything else I can help you with?"

"So does that mean you have a smaller Carver for sale?" Stephanie taunts him.

"Lady, I have work to do, so why don't you just look around. If you see anything that looks interesting, find me. My name is Danny."

"Really, would that be Danny Dykes? I think you were the guy I spoke to on the phone about a 46-foot Carver not too long ago."

All of a sudden, the man's face goes from tanned, to ashen, to red. He gives Stephanie a sinister look and reaches under the counter. However, before he can get whatever it is he is reaching for, Stephanie pulls a .25 caliber pistol from her pocket and points it at his nose. "I wouldn't do that if I were you, Danny."

She motions for him to come out from behind the counter. She takes a plastic tie from her purse and secures his hands behind his back. She walks over to the door and turns the open sign to closed, pulls down all of the blinds, and locks the door. She tells him to sit down. "Mr. Dykes, you and I are going to have a come-to-Jesus talk. I'm going to ask some questions and if you don't answer, I guess you already know what's going to happen next."

Chapter 23: Papa Boo's

The pressure on my trigger finger is increasing as I turn and confront my unknown guest. "Jake, what the hell are you doing? I could have shot you. Are you nuts?"

Jake had raised his hands very quickly and now was slowly lowering them. "Sorry, man. I came up here to spend some time thinking about Sissy and as I reached the top I saw you heading down this path."

"Well, why didn't you call out?"

"Chill out Mickke D, I said I was sorry. What are you doing over in this area anyway?"

I take a deep breath and place my weapon back into the small of my back. "I just wanted to clear my head and do a little exploring."

"Don't tell me you're still looking for that cave where the Indians and settlers stored all their provisions?"

"Of course not." I quickly change the subject. "Why aren't you working today?"

"Not much going on so I took the day off. What are you planning to do other than to try and find that cave?"

I give him a cold stare. "I was thinking about going back up to Buckeye Lake to check out some of the marinas to see if I can figure out who owns that antique Criss-Craft anchored out from The Winery. Do you want to go along?"

"Well, I guess. Do you have a bullet-proof vest I can wear?"

"Very funny. Let's go. You can buy lunch."

∂∽∾

We stop at three different marinas on the lake and no one seems to know who owns the boat, although everyone said they had seen the boat on the lake. I leave each of them a business card and ask them to call me if someone comes in with the boat.

We decide to stop at Papa Boo's for lunch. We are seated out near the lake and as we sit down, I turn and look out to where the boats are docked and I motion for Jake to look. The boat I have been searching for is moored at Papa Boo's boat dock.

Jake whispers, "Holy shit, Mickke D, do I need that vest now?"

"Take it easy, Jake; don't get your shorts in a knot. No one is going to try anything in a busy outdoor restaurant like this."

He smiles and says softly, "Does that include you?"

"Yes, that includes me. Now let's order lunch and we'll just keep an eye on the boat."

"Yea right. If I eat anything, I'll probably throw up."

As I scan the lunch bunch for any unsavory characters, I say, "Stay calm. We don't want to draw attention to ourselves."

I do notice a table on the far side of the eating area with two guys and a woman. The woman looks familiar, but until she stands up, I cannot be sure.

We order lunch along with a beer and enjoy the scenery and the surroundings. Fifteen minutes later, the three people at the suspect table get up and move toward the boat dock. The two men are unfamiliar to me. I grab my cell phone and snap several pictures as they are leaving. I try to take a good look at each of them just in case I run into them again. The woman almost looks like Ginny Ridlinger from Anchor Hocking. They all board that beautiful old antique boat. I notice the name on the back of the boat as it is leaving, "Black Gold." I quickly repeat the registration number on the boat and have Jake write it down. I get on my phone and call big Steve. "Say detective, I have more info on that boat I have been searching for. The registration number is OH56675IO and the name is "Black Gold." Can you see if you can find out who owns it?"

"I'll see what I can find out. Where are you?"

"Jake and I are having lunch at Papa Boo's."

Detective Reynolds does not answer. He just hangs up.

Chapter 24: The Interrogation

Stephanie walks over to the cooler and pulls out a Diet Pepsi in a plastic bottle. She takes off the cap, takes a drink, and pours the contents on the floor. "Oh, sorry Danny, that's going to be a sticky mess to clean up. Do you see this empty bottle?"

Danny does not answer, just nods his head. "Well Danny, this empty bottle is a poor man's silencer. Did you know that, Danny? All one needs to do is place this gun in the opening of the bottle, wrap some tape around it so it fits tight, and then fire. Hardly a sound. Would you like me to show you how it works? Let me see if I can find some tape in here somewhere."

With fear in his eyes and hesitation in his voice, Danny stammers, "Look lady, what do you want? Tell me what you want and I'll answer your damn questions."

"That's great, Danny. We are going to get along just fine. However, just in case you change your mind, I'm still going to find some tape and be ready to shoot you in the kneecap. Then I'll just get another bottle of Pepsi and we'll start over again with the other kneecap. Have you ever been shot in the kneecap Danny?"

"Damn it; tell me what you want to know." Danny is sweating profusely.

Stephanie walks back over to the cooler, gets out another bottle of Diet Pepsi, takes off the cap, takes a drink and pours the rest on the floor. She then looks around the office and finds some duct tape. "This will work great." She places the gun barrel in the bottle and wraps the duct tape around it until she has a tight seal.

Next, she walks behind the counter, reaches down and pulls out a .9mm Glock. "Whoa, nice gun. Maybe I'll use this one on your other kneecap."

She sits down across from him and begins. "Well, Danny. I sent you a beautiful 46-foot Carver along with three lovely women.

Those three ladies are now dead and I want to know what happened to them." She pauses and then starts again. "Danny, this is where you answer my question or I put a bullet in your kneecap."

Danny has been seriously considering his options and has decided the best thing he can do is truthfully answer this crazy woman's questions. He honestly believes she will kill him if he doesn't. However, before doing so he will make a bid to see if he can get a better deal. "Look lady, if I answer your questions, will you not kill me and at least give me a thirty-minute start before you call the authorities?"

She ponders the questions for a few seconds and then answers, "Danny, now you're making sense. If you answer my questions, I will be happy to give you a head start. I figure the authorities will catch you eventually, anyway. You have my word."

Danny begins. "Well, everything was fine until the State Police showed up and arrested me and a couple of guys just days after we had repainted the boat and changed the name and made some changes to the interior. I guess the owner of the boat had placed a GPS transponder somewhere on the boat and they tracked it to our location."

He pauses and Stephanie points the gun at his kneecap. "Don't stop now, Danny, you're doing fine."

"Well, so we are stuck with a $150,000 loan from some not very nice people as well as investing about $7,500 of our own money. We get out on bail and decide we had better find those women and see if we can get our money back."

"Who is 'We?' I need names."

"Harry Martin and Vandy Guthridge."

"And where might they be found?"

"Harry manages a strip club in Charleston and Vandy runs a charter fishing service not far from here. Harry was the one who found the financing for us and Vandy was the one who set up the rental boat to get the girls to Key West."

"Did you find the girls?"

"Yes, Vandy got in contact with his contacts in Key West where the girls dropped off the boat. One of them had a girlfriend who worked at the airport, and once he gave her their descriptions and about when they may have gone to the airport, she found where each of them had gone. We traced each of them to a different part of the Caribbean."

"And what happened once you found them?"

"Well, all I wanted to do was force them to give us the cash we had given them, but Vandy and Harry said they didn't want to leave any witnesses. They killed each of them after we found them and got whatever money we could get. I had nothing to do with the killing."

Stephanie's finger starts to put pressure on the trigger of her weapon but she eases off. She needs more information. "How much money did you get from them?"

"Let's see, altogether about $100,000, which we promptly paid to our banker. We still owe them almost $70,000, including interest."

"So Danny, where exactly do Harry and Vandy work?" She has a rather serene tone to her question.

"Harry is the manager of The Ultimate Gentleman's Club in Charleston and Vandy owns Local Deep Sea Fishing Charters about two miles south of here. I've answered all your questions, now can you just let me have a short head start before you call the cops?"

"You know what Danny, I've decided not to call the cops, and I lied about not killing you."

Danny gets a horrified look on his face but before he can scream, he is dead. The empty plastic bottle works well. There is hardly a sound.

Chapter 25: Kevin is Gone

Kevin has been taking his new pain pills for about three days now and they seem to be doing a great job of relieving his headache pain. The only downside is that his stomach has been acting up and he has lost his appetite as well. He has been thinking about what he should do about Donna Crist but he can't seem to come up with anything.

He leaves the office around five and just as he gets to his car, his cell rings. It's the unknown caller. "Kevin, I haven't heard any news about Donna Crist having had an accident. What are you waiting for?"

"Look, I have not been feeling well. My stomach has been upset. As soon as I get better, I'll take care of the problem."

The caller hesitates. "You know what, Kevin, why don't you come back up to the park and I will have some medicine for your stomach waiting for you, as well as some more pain pills. Look in the trash container again."

Kevin does not relish the drive back up to the park; however, the idea of more free pain pills overwhelms him.

He arrives at the park before six but has to wait in his car because several people are talking not far from the trash container. Five minutes later, they leave, and he hurries to the container and finds another plastic bag with a brown paper bag inside. He takes it back to his car and opens it. Inside he finds another container of pills and some sort of green liquid in a small plastic bottle. He takes the lid off and it smells like mint. He reads the note attached. It says to take two tablespoons twice a day. He feels so bad he decides to take a swig right now. He does so and his stomach does begin to feel better, almost a numbing sensation. He closes his eyes and leans his head back. Seconds later, he begins to cough, and spots of blood spew from his mouth and nose. Two minutes after that, he slumps over the steering wheel and dies.

The unknown caller, after seeing no one is around, walks over to the car and retrieves the bottle of pills, the plastic bottle with the green liquid, and the paper bag. He leaves several pain pills on the front seat, leaves the park, and thinks about another way to get rid of Donna Crist.

Chapter 26: Suicide or Murder

At eight that same evening, I get a call from big Steve. "I know who owns your mystery boat, but before I tell you, where were you between five and seven this evening?"

He catches me off guard with his question. "Well, let me think, I was in my room until about six and then I went downstairs and had dinner. Why are you asking?"

"I suppose someone can vouch for you being at dinner?"

"Detective, why are you asking me these questions, has something happened?"

"You might say that. The Sheriff's Department discovered an employee of the newspaper dead in his car just west of Pickerington. He was one of Sissy's assistant editors."

I hesitate and then ask, "Was his name Kevin?"

"Bingo. Did you know him?"

"I spoke with him several days ago about Sissy's computer but I did not know him. Was he murdered?"

"Not sure yet, but there were no wounds on the body. Could have been suicide or natural causes. They found prescription pain pills in the car. What were you trying to find out from him?"

"Donna Crist told me that he had told her that someone with a warrant came into the office the day after Sissy was found dead and took her computer. I was trying to find out who that was."

"Did he tell you?"

"No, said he had no idea who the person was and he abruptly ended our conversation. So tell me, who owns the boat?"

"It's registered to Wilmont Oil & Gas Company."

"Interesting. Thanks detective, got to go. I have another call coming in. I'll call you back?"

Donna is the new caller. She almost sounds like she's ready to cry. "I just heard from a friend at the newspaper that they found Kevin dead up around Pickerington. Have you heard anything?"

"Settle down Dee Dee, I just heard the news from my detective friend at the police department. Sounds like it could be suicide." I think for a few seconds and then ask, "Do you have someone you can visit out of town for a little while?"

"Why would I want to do that?" There's silence for several seconds. "Oh, my God, do you think he was murdered?" Donna has become hysterical. "Do you think someone may want to kill me?"

I try to reassure her, although diplomacy has never been one of my strong suits. "I didn't say that. I'm just saying why take a chance. Just go away for a couple of days until this case is solved or it blows over."

Donna eventually calms down. "I have a sister who lives up at Lakeside on Lake Erie. Maybe I'll go visit her for a few days. Will you call me and tell me when it is safe to come back?"

"You have my word, but I want you to pack up and leave tonight."

"Thanks Mickke D, I see why Sissy thought so much of you."

"So, now listen to me. Call me when you get there."

☙❧

Stuart Peterson easily finds out where Donna Crist lives and watches as she leaves her home with a small suitcase. Is this a planned road trip or did someone tell her about Kevin? He pulls out behind her and follows.

Chapter 27: Revenge #2

Stephanie ponders her next move as she quietly sits in her rented car in the parking lot of Local Deep Sea Fishing Charters. It's almost 7, it looks like the office is closed, and there are no vehicles in the parking lot. She figures the body of Danny Dykes won't be found until tomorrow morning, so she needs to complete her business tonight and get back to Antigua as soon as possible. She is feeling remorseful and responsible for the death of her friends because she had made the arrangements and sent them to the marina to sell TC's boat.

Just as she is about to start her car and leave, a car pulls into the parking area and the front door of the office opens. She slides down in her seat and peers over the steering wheel. A man appears from the office and walks toward the car. The man leans into the driver's side window and has a conversation with the driver. She can't see who is driving the car but the conversation becomes heated. The man pulls back from the car and the car quickly leaves the parking lot. The man yells something, gives the finger to the departing car, and then walks back toward the building.

Stephanie takes advantage of the situation and rolls down her window. She calls out, "Excuse me, is the office closed? I wanted to talk to someone about a charter."

The man turns, sees Stephanie, and answers, "Yeah, sure, come on in."

Stephanie follows the man into the building and he points to a chair in front of his desk. "So, what can I help you with?" he asks with a sly, leering grin on his face.

Stephanie frowns. "I wasn't sure you were open and I was about to leave when I saw that car come in and you came out of the building Mr.....?"

"Sorry, here's my card. Vandy Guthridge. Now what do you need, a short charter or an all-day one?"

"You didn't seem very happy with the person in that car. Is this a bad time?"

"Look lady, what can I do for you? I have places to go and people to see."

"Ok, Mr. Guthridge, or should I call you Vandy?"

He is getting impatient. "What the hell makes the difference; just tell me what you want."

"Well, Vandy this is not your lucky day. You see. I have come here to kill you just like you helped to kill those three girls who brought a 46-foot Carver to the marina a couple of months ago. Do you remember them?"

Vandy is speechless for several seconds. "What are you talking about lady, are you smoking wacky tabaccey?"

She pulls the Glock from her pocket and points it at him. "No Vandy, I'm fine. Do you recognize this gun? It used to belong to Danny but now Danny doesn't need it anymore."

"Holy shit. That's Danny's gun. Hey, Harry and Danny killed those girls. I had nothing to do with it."

"That's funny Vandy, because Danny said it was you and Harry. I'll just bet Harry will say it was you and Danny."

Stephanie pulls out the second empty soda bottle from the pocket of her light jacket and the duct tape. As she begins to tape the bottle around the weapon, Vandy starts to get up. "Sit down, Vandy."

Vandy sits down as Stephanie finishes her work. "Now you can get up." As he stands up, she pulls the trigger and puts a hole through his heart. He slumps back down in the chair. "Vandy, when you see Danny in hell, be sure and tell him the empty soda bottle still works. Hardly a sound."

She wipes down any prints she may have left and puts the "closed" sign on the inside of the door as she leaves. Next stop, Charleston.

Chapter 28: Call to Jim

My mind is going around in circles. Which direction do I go first? Kevin is dead, and I think Ginny Ridlinger is running around Buckeye Lake in a boat owned by Wilmont Oil & Gas. So, what has the director of public relations at Anchor Hocking have to do with Wilmont Oil & Gas? In addition, why was someone on that boat spying on me at The Winery the other night? In addition, did that have anything to do with someone sending Paul Bunyan and friends to pummel Jake and me?

It's time to give Jim another call. "Hey big guy, I need some more info on Von Spineback. See if you can find out if he was ever in the Armed Forces and if so, which branch."

He sarcastically answers, "No problem. How are things going up there? Shot anyone recently?"

"Very funny, keep that up and I'll forget about your OSU stuff."

"Oh don't do that, I'll get right back to you."

Ten minutes later, he calls back. "Von Spineback did a short tour in the Air Force. Anything else?"

"Thanks Jim, that will do for now."

I wonder if that's where Ginny met Von. Now I need to figure out if there is a relationship between the two.

One of the only things I have learned about women after being married to three of them is that they tell their hairdressers everything. Nothing is sacred when they're getting their hair done. I wonder who does Ginny's hair.

Chapter 29: Stuart Attacks

Stuart has been following Donna Crist at a safe distance for almost an hour on busy interstates and outer belts until she finally turns off on Route 4, a two-lane road leading north to Lake Erie.

Donna has been listening to classical music and thinking about different things she and her sister will do while visiting for a couple of days. She has no idea that the same set of headlights has been following her since she turned off on Route 4.

Stuart notices that traffic has almost disappeared on this straight stretch of highway. It is time to make his move. He eases his Hummer closer to his prey's vehicle, and when he sees no oncoming lights and nothing behind him, he pounces. He pulls out to pass and as his front right fender is close to her left rear fender, he bumps her car.

Donna is stunned. At sixty miles per hour, she has no time to react. Her vehicle all of sudden begins to spin and as her tires touch the loose gravel on the edge of the road, the car flips over and tumbles three or four times before coming to rest on its top in a ditch next to a fence.

Stuart slows and shines a spotlight located on the roof of his vehicle on the wrecked car. He notices a limp arm dangling from the driver's side shattered window and what looks like blood dripping down. He smiles and continues north for about a mile, turns around, and heads back toward the scene of the crash. He observes another vehicle at the crash scene. He figures he should stop and make sure she is dead but just as he slows down another vehicle pulls up. He does not slow down and continues on his way back to Columbus. He curses aloud. He should have made sure she was dead. About a mile down the road, he watches as an EMS vehicle and fire truck pass him and head toward the scene of the accident.

Chapter 30: Donna is Missing

It's 11:00 and I have not heard a word from Donna. She should have been there by now. I call her cell phone but no one answers. At 11:30, I call again but still no answer. I call big Steve, knowing he is going to read me the riot act.

"Mickke D, do you have any idea what time it is? Some of us have to get up early in the morning and go to work. What the hell do you want?"

"Sorry Steve, but I have been trying to call Donna Crist for the last hour and she doesn't answer her phone. I told her to leave town for a while and she was on her way to Lakeside up on Lake Erie. She was the one who told me about Kevin, and of course we know what happened to him."

"No Mickke D, we don't know what happened to him. He could have killed himself. And what do you expect me to do at 11:30 at night, go up to Lakeside and try to find her?"

I pause and then reply, "Hey detective, I'm sorry I bothered you." I hang up hoping he will call me back. I wait and wait and wait and now I'm not sure if I played this the right way.

Twenty minutes later, my phone rings. I was right. Big Steve was calling me back. "You knew I'd call back, didn't you?"

I hesitate and try to sound unconcerned. "No, but I was sure hoping you would. Did you find out anything?"

"I checked with the local Highway Patrol office and they said there was an accident on Route 4 about two hours ago. They found a car in the ditch on its top and the driver was identified as Donna Crist."

"Oh, my God, is she okay?" I ask with despair in my voice.

"She is alive but in serious condition. The doctors think she will make it."

"Thank God. Any idea what happened?"

"There were no witnesses and she has not gained consciousness. I'll let you know when I hear something."

It's time for a left jab. "Now do you believe me that there is something going on?"

He quickly counters, "Look, I'll admit things don't look right, but there is absolutely no hard evidence that a crime has been committed. Let's wait until I get the autopsy report on Kevin and then when we get a chance to talk to Donna Crist."

"Which hospital was she taken to? Do you have a guard with her?" I ask.

"She's at Doctor's Hospital in Bucyrus, and no they don't have a guard with her."

"Well, if I'm right and someone is trying to kill her, a guard would be a real good idea. If you're right then no guard is required, but what if you're wrong?"

"Okay, I'll call and have them post a guard at her room. Will that make you happy? Now can I go back to sleep?"

"Thanks, detective. I'll call you tomorrow."

I go directly to bed but sleeping does not come easy. I toss and turn most of the night. I get up and read for a while but that also doesn't work. Finally, about four in the morning I doze off. I have nightmares of claymore mines going off, of planes blowing up, and trucks slowly sinking in a swamp. I don't wake up until 10 the next morning when the maid knocks on my door. I am bathed in sweat. I yell at her, "please come back later!"

Chapter 31: Stuart is Back

After reading in the paper the next morning that Donna Crist was admitted to Doctor's Hospital in Bucyrus, Stuart decides to make a visit to the hospital to check on his still- alive victim. If he had only finished the job correctly last night, he would not have to be doing this now.

He arrives late morning and goes directly to the front desk. He is dressed in blue jeans, a sweatshirt, an Ohio State ball cap and large, black-rimmed glasses. He asks for information on Donna Crist. He is told that she is in Room 316 but that she is in serious condition and she is not allowed any visitors. He thanks the nurse for the information and walks over to the gift shop. He picks up several magazines to browse as he watches visitors and hospital personnel come and go. Then he notices an orderly go into the men's restroom who looks to be about his size.

He enters the restroom and the orderly is the only other person there. He quietly locks the bathroom door behind him and lies in wait for the man to depart the bathroom stall. The man finally opens the stall door and seems surprised to see someone else in the bathroom. Before he figures out what is going on, Stuart produces a switchblade knife and stabs the man in the abdomen, careful not to sever any major arteries. He doesn't want a lot of blood on the scrubs. He pushes the man back into the stall, stuffs his handkerchief in the man's mouth, and removes his scrubs. He puts the scrubs on over his street clothes. He closes the stall door, ties the man's hands and feet, leaves the bathroom, and walks up to the third floor. He figures fewer people will see him on the stairs than on the elevator.

He opens the third floor door and checks the signage on the wall to see which direction to go for Room 316. He follows the arrow, turns a corner, and abruptly stops. There is a uniformed officer sitting by the door to Room 316. The officer turns and looks his way.

Stuart never misses a beat. He waves at the officer and says, "Sorry officer, I got off one floor too soon." He decides that now is not the time to finish the job, although getting past this one guard would be simple. He doubts very much if Donna Crist saw him let alone is able to describe his vehicle. It won't be long before they discover the orderly's body in the bathroom and shut down the hospital. He retraces his steps and retreats back down the stairs to the ground floor, leaving the orderly's clothes in the second floor stairwell. Just as he is going out the front sliding-glass door of the hospital, he hears someone yell that there is blood on the floor of the men's restroom.

Chapter 32: Revenge #3

Stephanie arrives in Charleston and drives down River Street. The one-way, narrow, tree-lined avenue has vehicles parked on both sides. There is barely enough room to navigate with her medium-sized car. She can see the flashing neon sign noting the club ahead, and just as she begins to wonder where in the world she is going to park, a car pulls out not half a block from the club. She quickly secures the parking spot.

She leaves the .9mm Glock in the glove compartment and places her small, .25 caliber weapon in a concealed pocket in her purse. She watches as several people enter the club. The men are patted down and the women are asked to open their purses so the door attendant can check for weapons. Some of the women just hand the purse to the man and others, not willing to part with their highly prized possession, open the purse for him to gaze in to its dark confines with a small flashlight.

She puts on her wig and glasses and exits the car. The line to get in the club thins as she nears the door. The door attendant, who reminds her of Tarzan on steroids with his long, flowing hair and body-builder type physique, asks to see her purse. She does not offer the clutch bag but holds it open instead. As long as she can hold the purse, Tarzan will not notice the weight of the gun. He motions her on as she asks in her best American accent, "Is Harry here tonight?"

He responds in broken English with a Russian inflection, "Yeah, I think so. Check with Patz at the bar."

"Did you say Patsy?"

"No, I say Pat Z, you don't understand English?"

"Gotcha, Patz. Thank you." She is thinking to herself, *I may cut your hair before I leave here, you condescending Russian baby ape.*

She moves into the dimly lit building and after her eyes adjust to the darkness, she spots the bar, ventures down to the far end, and sits on a bar stool. A very attractive young girl with short shorts and only smiley pasties with tassels covering the nipples of her perky, eye-catching bare breasts comes over.

"The doorman said to ask for Patz, is that you?"

"That's me, what would y'all like to drink?"

Stephanie is considering asking her if her mother knows she dresses like this and telling her she should put some clothes on, when all of a sudden, the music starts and three stages are immersed in spotlights. Three lovely girls come out dressed in a lot less than Patz the bartender, and each begins having a love affair with a highly polished silver pole.

"Sorry, first time here. I'll have a draft. Is Harry in?" she stammers.

"Is he expecting y'all? Do y'all have an appointment?" Patz replies in a thick Southern drawl.

"Could you tell him Danny from the marina sent me over?"

"Sure hon, let me give him a call."

She turns her back to Stephanie, walks down to the other end of the bar, and makes a call on her cell phone. After a few seconds, she returns. "He'll be right down darlin'. Did y'all say you wanted a draft?" Stephanie nods her head in agreement.

Patz returns with the beer. "Do y'all want to pay for this now or start a tab?"

"I'll pay now, how much?"

"That will be eight dollars, darlin'."

She thinks to herself, *Eight dollars for a glass of beer. Maybe I should invest in a strip club,* as she places a ten on the bar.

She sips on the watered-down beer. Five minutes later, Harry shows up. She can tell he is not very impressed with her wig and glasses look. "You the girl Danny sent over?"

"That is me, he said you might have a job opening. I just moved into town and stopped at the marina to see if anything was available there. Danny told me to stop at the charter fishing office just down the road and talk to Vandy, and then come on down here and talk to you. Vandy wasn't in so here I am."

Danny looks her up and down and replies, "Well, you sure don't look like the dancer type unless you're hiding something under those clothes. By the way, I called Danny at the office and on his cell phone and he doesn't answer."

Stephanie conjures up a puzzled look and replies, "Well, I just left there about an hour ago. He was definitely there when I left."

"Okay, come on up to my office and we'll talk, but I'm not promising anything."

Stephanie peers at him and then at Patz. "Well I guess I can do that. Do you by chance have a soft drink in a plastic bottle I can take with me?"

"Sure hon, I've got a Diet Coke, will that do?"

"That will work just fine."

Patz returns with the drink, sets it on the bar, and says, "That will be five dollars."

Stephanie gazes at Harry and he just shrugs his shoulders. She lays a five on the bar and the two ones she got in change from the beer and sarcastically says, "Thanks for all your help, Patz."

"You're welcome, darlin', and thanks for pronouncing my name correctly. Most people call me Patsy or pasty."

Stephanie opens her mouth to say something but thinks better and just smiles. She follows Harry around the corner and up a flight of stairs to a large, nicely decorated office with a window overlooking the main floor. She makes note that even in the office the decibel levels from the music are still high. She opens the Diet Coke and takes a long drink.

Harry, with both hands in a prayer position under his chin, asks, "So what do I call you, sweetie? You sure are a tall drink of water."

Stephanie has always hated the fact that everyone in South Carolina either refers to you as sweetie, honey, darlin', or luv. "You know, I hate being called sweetie. How about just calling me Steph?"

"Hey, don't be so bitchy, Steph, remember you're the one looking for a job."

"Well, you see Harry, I sort of lied about the job thing. I actually just wanted to get you alone somewhere."

Harry smiles. "So, what did you have in mind?"

Stephanie smiles back, pulls the gun from her purse, and points it at him. "This is what I have in mind, Harry. Now do what I say. Put both hands palm down on your desk and don't say a word, just listen." She takes another long swig of Diet Coke and pours the remainder on the lush carpet on Harry's floor.

"What the hell are you doing, you crazy bitch? How did you get that gun in here?"

"Now Harry, I thought I told you not to talk. Danny and Vandy talked too much and now they are both dead. Before they died, they told me that it was your idea to kill the three girls who brought you guys the 46-foot Carver from Pawleys Island."

Harry suddenly stands up, keeping his palms on the desk, and says loudly, "I don't know what you're talking about. You had better get out of here before I call the cops."

"Sorry, Harry, but I don't believe you." She jams the gun into the empty plastic bottle as far as she can and pulls the trigger. It's not quite as noiseless as having the bottle taped to the gun but almost. The bottle flies across the room as Harry crumbles to the floor, a bullet hole in his forehead.

Stephanie closes the door as she leaves the office and waves at Patz as she departs the club.

Patz calls out, "Hope you get the job."

"Yeah, me too sweetie."

As she leaves the club, the door attendant asks her if she found Patz. "I certainly did. Thank you so much for all your help." She takes two steps, turns, and says, "Now go get a haircut."

The attendant gives her the finger as she turns and continues on her way.

She drives back to her hotel and has no problem getting a good night's sleep knowing that in some small way she has avenged the murder of her three friends. She opts to catch a boat back to Bermuda the following morning and then island hop back to Antigua. She plans to return after things settle down a bit. She will then pursue the maps in Georgetown and find the buried treasure. She pitches the unloaded .9mm Glock in a retention pond outside of her hotel and, after wiping away any fingerprints, places the .25 caliber gun in an oilcloth and plastic bag. She buries it in a flowerpot at the hotel. She hopes it will still be there when she returns.

Chapter 33: The Day Spa

I am just about to start calling beauty salons in Lancaster when my phone rings. It's TC. "You're not going to believe what's going on down here. Are you sitting down?"

"Yes, I am. What's up? Did you figure out where the treasure is buried?"

"No, I'm afraid not, but three men were killed yesterday, or should I say murdered. Guess who they were?"

"TC, I have no idea, so why don't you just tell me."

"The three guys who were arrested for trying to sell my boat in Charleston."

"You mean they weren't in jail?"

"No, they were all out on bond. But wait, it gets better. Guess who I thought I saw yesterday in Murrells Inlet?"

"I have no idea."

"Stephanie."

"You're kidding. Stephanie Langchester?"

"Yes, our Stephanie."

"No TC, not our Stephanie. You hired her, not me. Have the authorities ever found or heard from her or the other three girls?"

"Don't know, no one has contacted me," he replies.

"Okay, let me call Jim at the office and have him see what he can find out from his FBI friends. I'll let you know. In the meantime, be careful."

"No problem. Have Jim call me if he needs any info on them."

I immediately call Jim. "Hey big guy, are you on the golf course?"

"No, I am not on the golf course. Why does everyone think I play golf every day?"

I chuckle. "I have no idea. Hey, I need you to check with your sources and see what you can find out about the four girls who worked for TC on the salvage job in Pawleys Island. Call him if you need information. There's a file on my desk with their names. Let me know what you find out, and before you ask, I have not got your OSU shirts yet but I will."

∂∞⊸

While I'm waiting for Jim to call me back, I figure I will begin calling around town to beauty shops to see if by chance I can find out some gossip on Ms. Ridlinger. My story is going to be that I want to surprise my girlfriend with a complete spa makeover and I don't want her to know about it.

Fortunately, on only my fifth call, I hit pay dirt. "This is The Beauty Day Spa, Beth Bryan speaking, how can I help you?"

"Hi, Beth, I'm a friend of Ginny Ridlinger and I wanted to know if by chance she might be a client of yours?"

Beth does not answer immediately but finally says in a cautious sort of way, "And why would you like to know that?"

"Oh, I'm sorry Beth, I'm, you might say, a close friend of hers, and I wanted to get her a gift card for a spa treatment and makeover but I wanted it to be a surprise so I couldn't ask her where she gets her hair done. What's your best deal?"

The thought of a big sale loosens her lips. "Oh, you must be that well-off oil guy she's been telling me about."

Touchdown! I quickly reply, "Now Beth, we don't want to start spreading rumors, do we?"

"No sir, what takes place in the beauty salon, stays in the beauty salon. Our best deal and one I know Ginny will love is the CEO Treatment. It runs $450 but worth every penny."

"Well Beth, that's the one I want. Where are you located? I'll stop by tomorrow afternoon to pick it up."

Beth gives me the address, which I repeat as if I am writing it down, and I remind her not to mention this to Ginny. I now have my answer. Ginny and Von Spineback know each other very well and they were both in the Air Force. So I wonder what the link is between Wilmont Oil & Gas Company and Anchor Hocking.

∂∞⊸

Thirty minutes later, Jim calls back. "Here's what I found. Stephanie has not surfaced but the other three girls are dead, murdered. According to my people, British Intelligence thinks Stephanie, who once worked for them, killed the girls, and they are looking for her."

"Thanks Jim, that answers my question."

かめめ

That same afternoon, Ginny Ridlinger shows up for her 3 o'clock appointment at The Beauty Day Spa. By 3:30, Beth Bryan can't stand the pressure any longer. She tells Ginny all about her conversation on the phone with Mr. "Big Spender" and makes Ginny promise to act surprised and not to tell him she told her.

Ginny knows that her friend would never call the beauty shop. In fact, he made it very clear; not to mention their relationship in public, at least not yet. All of their public appearances, which have been few and far between, have always been outside of Lancaster. She asks Beth if by chance her office phone would show the number of the caller. Beth brings it up and shows it to Ginny.

"Yep, that's him," Ginny lies, knowing that the number does not belong to her significant other and benefactor but to the private investigator from Myrtle Beach.

As soon as Ginny gets into her car, she calls Von Spineback and breaks the news about the PI calling the beauty shop trying to find out if she was hooked up with him. Von is not a happy camper, "And how did your beautician know you were seeing me?"

"Von, I never mentioned your name. I only said I was seeing a guy in the oil business."

"Well, we can't let anything slow us down until the sale goes through, so I guess I'll have Stu have a talk with our PI friend."

Chapter 34: Rhubarb

My phone won't stop ringing. This time it's big Steve. "Mickke D, I just got the results from the autopsy on that Kevin fellow. He was poisoned. The M.E. found large traces of rhubarb leaves in his system, as well as several pain pills. Rhubarb itself is fine to eat but the leaves are toxic as hell. Now we have a murder, and since the deed happened in the county, the Sheriff's Department is handling the case."

"My God, why would anyone eat rhubarb leaves if they're poisonous?"

"The M.E. thinks he may have ingested something that had been laced with extract from the leaves. He found a green substance with a mint smell to it among his stomach contents. Without an autopsy, the cause of death would have just been an overdose since they found pain pills in the car."

"So where do we go from here, detective?" I ask, already knowing the answer.

"We don't go anywhere. It's the Sheriff's case now."

"What about Donna Crist? Have you heard anything about her condition?"

"She's still in serious condition and there is a guard on her room. I'll let you know the minute I hear anything. Why don't you just go back to Myrtle Beach and let the authorities handle this? By the way, I'm sending over a copy of that file you wanted. Turtle, I'm sorry, I mean Officer Tom Barrish will deliver it to you."

"Turtle?" I blurt out.

"Long story, don't ask," he replies.

"Thanks, Steve. Can't wait to look it over. I think I'll stay around for a while. I'm still looking into the death of Sissy's husband five years ago. But I will stay out of their way. Let me know if I can help." I end the call before he can answer.

Within minutes, there is a knock at my door. I grab my .45 from the bedside table and quietly go over to the door. I look through the peephole. I see a uniformed officer on the other side of the door. I move away from the door and ask, "Who is it?"

"Detective Reynolds sent me over with an envelope for you."

"What's your name officer?" I learned a long time ago that one could never be too careful.

"Officer Barrish."

I replace my weapon on the table and open the door. The officer hands me the envelope and asks me to sign a receipt, which I do. I thank him and close the door.

I take out the copied file and begin to read. The M.E. found no bruises or trauma to the woman's body. He found water in her lungs so she didn't die before she ended up in the tub. There was a half-empty bottle of vodka on the table with her fingerprints all over it. Her stomach was full of pain pills. She had checked in alone. The detective in charge of the crime scene had made two notes, which he included in his report. 1) There was no suicide note, and 2) her cell phone is missing.

The final sentence in the report said that they interviewed her pain management doctor and he checked out okay. His name was Dr. Jon Spineback.

Bingo! Dr. Jon Spineback's name pops up again.

Chapter 35: Von's Plan

Von Spineback has been looking for the big "gusher" for twenty years, as has every person who has ever been in the exploration field of the oil and gas industry. Three years ago, Wilmont Oil & Gas drilled a test well in Fairfield County, and the results made Wilmont's 270 leases consisting of 27,543 acres in the county priceless. They drilled two more exploratory wells on the fringes of the lease block with the same impressive results. Only the geologist and the drilling supervisor know the results besides him. Von sent several landmen out into the county to acquire as many leases as possible to protect the boundaries of his find. As far as the public is concerned, the wells are marginal at best.

Von figures there are literally millions of barrels of oil and millions of cubic feet of natural gas under his block of leases. The problem is getting the oil and natural gas to market. His original thought was to build a pipeline, but that would take too long and would be very expensive as well as environmentally dangerous. He doesn't need tree huggers slowing down his project. He looked around the county and found the perfect answer to his problem. Anchor Hocking's Distribution Center along with 182 acres on West Fair Avenue would easily solve the problem. The plant has everything he needs: size, location, and rail availability.

He only has five years remaining on the majority of his undrilled leases so he needs to get the ball rolling. He needs to drill or renew the leases. If he begins that process, everyone in Fairfield County will figure out Von's discovery wells are more than marginal. This will bring about a leasing frenzy in Fairfield County. The price to renew his leases will go sky high and cost his company millions.

He accidently ran into Ginny Ridlinger in Columbus, and when he discovered she was working as the director of public relations at the distribution center in Lancaster, he was elated. After resurrecting their old Air Force affair and the promise of a big payout to Ginny, he now had an inside edge with the company.

His plan, along with some inside help from Ginny, is to purchase the distribution plant through a dummy corporation, claiming they can run the distribution center more efficiently than Anchor, and then close it down. Later, the dummy corporation will transfer the property to Wilmont Oil & Gas. He will then cover the acreage with huge storage tanks for the oil. He will truck the oil from each well site to the central storage tanks on West Fair Avenue. Tanker trucks will then haul the oil to refineries or it will be loaded on to railroad cars for distribution. He plans to set up a natural gas pipeline station on the property and sell his gas to the nearest pipeline, which is only one mile away. He is already in the process of acquiring rights of way for the pipeline. He wants to get the rights of way before he shuts down the plant so that none of the landowners who may work at the plant can block his route.

If his plan goes through, more than 500 workers at the distribution plant will lose their jobs. If the distribution plant is closed, Anchor will need to find another place for their distribution or, as Sissy Adams feared, it would have to close the two manufacturing plants in town, which would put another 3,000 workers out of jobs. This could be the straw that breaks the back of the already financially troubled company and the economy of Lancaster.

Von Spineback really doesn't care and he is not going to let one PI from Myrtle Beach stand in his way. Von calls Stu and gives him the okay to terminate the PI. Stu gives him an update on Donna Crist and tells Von he will take care of both situations.

Chapter 36: Big Ed Connehey

Immediately after reading the police report, I call Detective Ed Connehey with the Reynoldsburg Police Department. I get lucky. He's in the office. "This is big Ed, Homicide, how can I help you?"

"Big Ed?" I'm caught off guard. All I can think of is big Steve.

"It's an office name, long story. How can I help you?"

"Detective, my name is Mickke MacCandlish and I'm a private investigator from Myrtle Beach, South Carolina, and if you have a few minutes I would like to talk to you about an OD case you were on about five years ago."

"Mr. MacCandlish, I've been on a lot of overdose cases, you're going to have to be a little more specific."

"The OD victim was Sue Ellen North, wife of state representative Michael North. Do you remember the case?"

There is silence on the other end of the line. "Detective Connehey, are you still there?"

"Mr. MacCandlish, what is a private investigator from Myrtle Beach doing looking into the overdose death of Sue Ellen North?"

"Well actually, I'm up here looking into the death of the sister of a friend of mine. She died after falling from Mt. Pleasant a couple of weeks ago. My friend is her brother and he thinks she was murdered. Did you read about it in the paper?"

"I think I vaguely remember the story, but what do these two cases have to do with each other?"

"Detective, there is one glaring similarity. In each case the victim's cell phones were missing and never found."

Detective Connehey pauses before continuing. "Mr. MacCandlish, before I say anything else, is there someone who can vouch for you that I can talk to?"

"Sure detective, you can call Detective Steve Reynolds with the Lancaster Police Department." I give him Steve's cell phone number and he says he will call me back.

Forty-five minutes later, he calls. "Well, I spoke with Detective Reynolds and he sort of vouched for you. He said you were a pain in the ass but probably honest. He also said you were ex-Special Forces. Is that true?"

"Yes it is. You too?"

"Yes sir, and I remembered your name after Detective Reynolds said Mickke D. We had a class one day on some things one should never do during a mission and you were the first one mentioned. Something about turning claymores around on a cocaine encampment in Colombia. Was that you?"

"Yeah, that was me. I was hoping that little incident had been forgotten. Who was giving the class, Colonel Townsend?"

"Yes, it was, and I called him to check on you as well." He laughs. "He also told me that there were some other crazy things you had done after Special Forces, but they were classified. So Mickke D, what do you need to know about the Sue Ellen North case?"

Feeling more relaxed and happy to get back to the case, I reply, "What was your opinion of her pain management doctor, Jon Spineback?"

Detective Connehey thinks for a minute before answering. "I would say very well rehearsed. He had all the correct answers as if he knew what the questions were going to be, and he wasn't that concerned that his patient was dead."

"Did he have an alibi for the night she died?"

"Oh yes, and the pills found in the room were not prescriptions he had written for her. We had no reason to go any further with the investigation. You might say he had all of his ducks in a row. Is he a suspect in your case?"

"He may be. By the way, did you know he had a twin brother Von?"

"No, that never came up."

I think of another question to ask Detective Connehey. "When you talked with her husband, did he know she was hooked on pain pills?"

"He knew she was taking pain pills but he had no idea she may have been addicted to them. He was devastated."

"Did he know Dr. Spineback?"

"I don't think so but he said his wife seemed happy with him."

It's time for me to move on. "Thank you, Detective, you've been very helpful."

"No problem. Call if you need anything else. If you're ever up this way, I would love to meet you."

"Thanks. I'll keep that in mind." I feel good knowing I probably have another inside source in a police department.

Now I think it's time to have a talk with the twins.

Chapter 37: Dr. Jon Spineback

The following morning, I call Dr. Jon Spineback's office in Reynoldsburg and speak with his receptionist. I tell her that I am in a lot of pain with a bad back, and that I would like to get in to see the doctor as soon as possible. She checks her appointment book and tells me she has a cancellation at 11:30. I give her a fake name and tell her I will be there.

I arrive with a noticeable limp around 11:15 and begin filling out my forms. It's kind of fun to make up all of this stuff and when she asks for my insurance card, I tell her I will pay with cash. When she asks for my driver's license and Social Security number, I tell her I forgot and left them at home. She frowns but tells me to have a seat, that the doctor will be right with me.

Ten minutes later, I am ushered into one of those small, cold exam rooms with uncomfortable chairs. The nurse asks me some questions and takes my blood pressure, then quickly retreats and says the same thing; the doctor will be in shortly. That's when I notice magazines spread out on a table. I figure that means it may be awhile. I am right. Twenty minutes later, in walks Dr. Jon Spineback.

Dr. Jon is an intimidating looking man. He is about 5'10 or 5'11, bald, and I can tell even through his white medical frock that he works out regularly and may have been a wrestler or weightlifter in his younger days. Suddenly, I remember where I have seen him - at Papa Boo's on Buckeye Lake. He was one of the guys with Ginny Ridlinger, or maybe that was his twin brother Von. He does not offer to shake my hand.

"Mr. Candish (my made up name), what seems to be your problem? I see here," gazing at his clipboard, "you have no insurance and no driver's license or Social Security number."

"Well, Doc, I have a bad back and I would like some pain pills. I was told I could get some here. Can you fix me up?"

I notice he is taking a closer look at me, as if he has seen me before, "I don't know who told you that, Mr. Candish, but I just don't dole out pain pills to every Tom, Dick and Harry who walks in the door."

It's time to hit him hard and hit him fast. "Actually doc, my name is Mickke MacCandlish and I don't have a bad back." I hand him my card, which he reluctantly accepts. "I'm a private investigator from Myrtle Beach and I would like to ask you some questions about the death of Sue Ellen North and the death of David Adams. Both of them died about five years ago."

I notice a slight twinge of pink creeping into his cheeks, but he quickly regains his composure. "Mr. MacCandlish, or whatever your name is, Sue Ellen North was a patient of mine but I know nothing about her tragic overdose and I do not know a Mr. Adams. I would appreciate it if you would leave so I can take care of some real patients who need my help." He turns and moves towards the door.

"No problem, doc. Say, didn't I see you on Allen Road last Saturday? You were in a black SUV."

Turning back, a soft smile comes over his face. "Sorry, Mr. MacCandlish, I was out of town last weekend."

"How about Buckeye Lake two days ago?"

"Wrong again, Mr. MacCandlish; I've never been to Buckeye Lake. Now please leave or I will call the authorities." For the first time, I notice anxiety in his voice.

As I leave the office, my instincts are telling me this man is hiding something. I need to go back and check the notes from Sissy. I can't remember a Dr. Spineback on her list.

❧❦

Dr. Jon goes back to his office and dials a number on his cell phone. "Stu, it's Dr. Jon. I need a problem taken care of right away."

He tells Stu about his conversation with the PI and gives him his name.

"No problem Dr. Jon. I think I'll enjoy this one. I'll bill you when I'm finished." Stu is laughing to himself. He will get paid twice for eliminating the same person. It doesn't get any better than this. He is already conceiving ways to eliminate both of the brothers' problems.

Stu is working for both Dr. Jon and Von Spineback, but the brothers don't know that. Dr. Jon uses him to collect from pill pushers who do not pay up or short him on their payment.

Chapter 38: Beverly

Beverly Beery has finally received the phone call she has been hoping for. Her boss Liz Woodkark called this morning and told her she was good to go on her trip to the Caribbean. Her plane ticket is on the way, as well as a new passport and drivers license with the name Cathy Mars on them. She has a one-way ticket to the Bahamas with an open-end return. Included will be instructions where weapons may be acquired and any other materials she may need, as well as an 8 X 10 photo of her target. Although it may sound like a vacation, Beverly realizes it is actually work. She has a unique job. She finds people for her boss and sometimes eliminates them.

Liz is an employee with the Department of Defense in Washington, D.C., but her real job is to run a rogue cell operation for the CIA. She and her group take care of problems in society that the courts and law enforcement fail to enforce or control. She answers only to the Director of the CIA, and usually it's only when she initiates the call. When a new director comes in, he or she is lightly informed of Liz and her group. Liz uses third parties, code words, and code names so that even the people she is talking to don't really know who she is or what she does. She is funded through materials confiscated from drug dealers and other wanted persons. Taxpayer money does not fund her projects. There is no money trail back to her group.

Beverly's new job will be to find Stephanie Langchester, a former British Intelligence agent who they suspect killed three women who were working with her on a salvage job in Myrtle Beach, South Carolina. British Intelligence contacted Liz through a third party in Canada and asked if she could help. Liz accepted the mission. She was told that British Intelligence thinks she may be in the Caribbean. Liz negotiated a healthy fee for her services.

For now, all Liz wants is for Beverly to find Stephanie. A decision to eliminate her will be considered later. She warns her to be careful, that Stephanie is probably armed and very dangerous. Beverly has a plan in mind. She will make copies of the photo she received from Liz of Stephaine. She plans to post them in different regions of the Caribbean. She will state on the photo that this is her missing sister and will mention a small reward. Either someone will come forward with a sighting or Stephanie herself may show up. Either way, Beverly's plan will be a success.

Chapter 39: Stuart is Back

I spend the rest of the day going over Sissy's notes. She did not interview a Dr. Jon Spineback; however, I did find a Jon Spineback on big Steve's list of black SUV owners who live in Live Oak Estates. The doctor she interviewed was a Dr. Lyndon Johnson, and she seemed to think he was legit.

Dr. Johnson was indeed legit, and in a casual conversation at lunch one day with several other doctors, including Dr. Spineback, he had told the group about his interview with Sissy. He said she was going after the bad guys, the ones who give their profession a bad name, which should make everyone happy. He did not make Dr. Jon happy.

I fall asleep in one of the cozy chairs in my room. When I wake up, it's dark outside. My stomach is growling so I head out to get a good hamburger, maybe a Jimmy's Jawbreaker. Jake told me I could still get one and where they were located.

Shaw's lot was full when I returned last night so I had parked in the public parking area behind the hotel. There had been a light rain during the day and the pavement is still wet. As I approach my vehicle, for some reason I notice what looks like some sort of flashing light in a puddle on the wet pavement coming from under my vehicle. I get down on my hands and knees and carefully look under the SUV. Holy shit, there's a bomb under my car, and the flashing light is green. Instinctively, I get up and begin to run when

I see two couples walking my way. I yell, "Run, run the other way, there's a bomb!" They all turn and run with me.

Seconds later, I guess the green light turned to red because there was a huge explosion and my brand-new SUV turned into a piece of molten metal. We are all thrown to the ground by the force of the blast. I ask if they are all right and they answer affirmatively.

Just as we begin to stand up, several shots ring out and bullets ricochet off the paved parking lot and into the metal sides and tires of cars around us. I yell to get behind a vehicle and get down. They heed my warning immediately. I draw my weapon and look for a target.

As quickly as the shots rang out, they end just as quickly. The only sounds we hear are the roaring flames from my SUV and several other cars in the lot that are now on fire, along with several vehicle horn alarm systems set off from the force of the blast. Then another fierce explosion erupts as the fire reaches one of the gas tanks from a burning car. I motion for my group to stay down.

The next sound we hear is welcome. Sirens are coming our way. I slowly stand up, and no shots are fired so the others stand up as well and we all survey the noisy war zone. It is not a pretty sight. Fire trucks, EMS and the police all arrive about the same time. The fires are extinguished without much trouble and some of the horns eventually stop sounding their blaring warnings.

I, as well as the two couples, am examined by the EMTs. No one seems physically hurt, but I think they will have a hard time sleeping for a while. Their entire lives have been changed in about two minutes. They will live in fear for several months or maybe longer. They will jump at the sound of a loud noise, and they will continually be looking over their shoulders. They may even look under their cars before getting in them for months or maybe years to come. They could be considered civilian war casualties. I know because I've been there in that dark place, but I was trained to get over it. However, I don't believe one ever gets over it, you just learn to accept it and move on.

None of them say much; they just shake their heads when questioned by the police. They look my way and give a half-wave as if to say thanks. Finally, both couples walk over and introduce themselves as the Courtwrights and the Shorts. They all thank me for what I did. I thank them and tell them it was nothing heroic, just a gut reaction. Just then, an officer comes over to question me. Before he can begin, I hear a familiar voice behind me. "I'll question this one, officer." It's big Steve and as usual where I'm involved, he is not a happy camper. "Mickke D, what the hell have you done now?"

"What have I done?" For a split second, I almost forget he is a friend and consider smashing my fist into his face, but the thought quickly passes. I take a deep breath and calmly reply, "Well for starters, I probably saved those two couples over there from being blown up by a car bomb placed under my vehicle."

He waves at the four civilians and I'm not sure he knows how to continue. "Whatever. Tell me what happened," he replies with a frown as the last of the horns stop honking. The air is suddenly quiet but filled with the smells of burning metal, gasoline, and the stench of terror.

As he takes notes, I replay the entire moments before and after the first blast. I include the fact that someone was also firing a weapon at us. "It sounded like an AR-15 on automatic and I think it was coming from that building." I point to what looks like a vacant building about a hundred yards away. "So, do you now believe I've opened up a can of worms and that someone murdered Sissy Adams and maybe her husband David, or do you still not have enough evidence?"

With arms folded across his chest, he replies slowly and quietly, "I think you and those folks over there are very lucky to be alive, and yes, I am probably going to re-open Sissy's case."

"Well, detective, at least that's a beginning." I walk away and over toward the remains of my brand-new vehicle. Detective Reynolds does not follow. I gaze at what's left of my SRX and then turn back, and walk back to where big Steve is standing. With as serious a look on my face as I can muster I say, "Steve, I need an automatic rifle."

∞

Stuart can't believe he pushed the wrong button on his cell phone and gave the PI just enough time to escape. He cleans up the brass on the rooftop and disappears before the authorities arrive.

Chapter 40: Donna Wakes Up

In Bucyrus, Donna Crist finally opens her eyes, is alert, and taken off the serious list. She has a broken arm, cuts and bruises, and a concussion. The doctor says she should be released within a couple of days. The authorities question her, but she can't remember much of anything about the crash and has no idea what type of vehicle hit her.

She asks for her cell phone and one of the nurses brings it to her. Thank goodness she brought along her charger as well. The nurse plugs it in for her and the first person she calls is her sister at Lakeside. Her sister had no idea why she didn't show up and why she has been unable to contact her. She tells Donna that she will be down to pick her up.

The second person she calls is Mickke D. "Well, I never made it to Lakeside."

He replies, "Yeah, I know. Glad to hear you're still among the living. I talked them into putting a guard on your room. Do you remember anything about the accident?"

"No, not a thing. They want to release me in a day or two. Where should I go?"

He thinks about that for a few seconds and then says, "I think you should go on to your sister's. Can she pick you up? By the way, does your sister have a different last name?"

"That should not be a problem, and yes she has a different last name."

"That's good. I will speak to the locals and make sure you go out a back entrance so as not to be spotted in case someone is watching for you. I'll make all the arrangements and then you need to call me when you get to the lake."

He calls the local authorities in Bucyrus. Big Steve had told them that he might be contacting them. He asks them to post a release date for Donna and then have her really leave the day before and not out the front door. They agree, although they would have liked to set a trap for the person who attacked the hospital employee and was probably after Donna.

∂∽∾

Stu is back in Bucyrus at the crack of dawn on the day Donna is to be released. He is very upset when she never walks out the front door. He wants to go in but decides it would be too risky. He also notices several people who look like undercover cops patrolling the area. He now turns his attention back to the PI. He will deal with Donna Crist later.

Chapter 41: Offense

After a mostly sleepless night, I call my insurance company the first thing the next morning. I need a means of transportation. They agree to rent me a car and replace my SRX before I head back to the beach. They want me to send them a police report about the accident. I call big Steve and he says he will fax the report to my insurance company. He also tells me he approved my borrowing an AR-15 and some ammo from the police weapons room. All I need to do is to stop by and sign for it. He warns me in a pleading sort of way to please not shoot any civilians.

About an hour later, a rental company drops off a Chevy Impala. I go directly to the police department and sign for my weapon. They give me a receipt so I can show I have proof to have the weapon in my possession. I place the weapon in the trunk of the Impala. I lock and load a full clip of ammo in the rifle and place three more full clips where I can get to them in a hurry. I am tempted to go on up to Reynoldsburg and stick the rifle up the nose of Dr. Spineback, but instead, I opt to go have a nice late breakfast. While enjoying my meal, I start to put a plan together to find out which brother is trying to kill me. Then all of a sudden, after biting into a delicious crispy piece of bacon, it hits me. *What if both of them are after me? What if one of them killed Sissy and the other one killed David?*

I don't see Dr. Spineback doing the everyday grunt work of killing someone, although Detective Connehey in Reynoldsburg seems to think he had a hand in the killing of Sue Ellen North. I also do not believe he would have the ability to put together the bomb I saw under my vehicle. That took someone with a military or government black ops background. So if he isn't my attempted killer, then who is?

I get out my phone and go back to the pictures I took at Papa Boo's at Buckeye Lake. I send them off to Jim in Myrtle Beach and ask him to see if any of his friends at the bureau might be able to recognize any of the people in the pictures.

∂∞∾

Jim calls me thirty minutes later. "Well, boss, I have good news and bad news. The good news is that my friends at the bureau recognized only one of the people in your photos, and the bad news is that he is a real bad ass. His name is Stuart Peterson and he has been listed as a person of interest in several murders in the central Ohio area, but no one has come up with enough evidence to arrest him or indict him."

"Who was murdered?" I ask.

"They were all drug dealers and pimps."

"So did they give you any background information on the guy?"

"Sure did. He's an ex-CIA intelligence officer. He was asked to leave the CIA after several prisoners in Afghanistan died while being interrogated by him. He also has a degree in computer science. He landed in the central Ohio area about five years ago and runs a computer consulting business out of a small storefront in Reynoldsburg. No arrests or convictions on his record. The CIA gave the bureau a heads up on this guy in case they ever ran into him."

"Interesting. That's the same time frame when one of my victims was killed. So why is he a person of interest with the bureau?"

"Don't know. I am going to guess that part of his file is confidential. I would guess he is on their watch list."

"Thanks, Jim. Email me the computer store address. Maybe I'll stop in and see if he can fix my laptop. How about notifying your friends at the bureau that I may be stopping by and not to panic just in case they have eyes on him?"

"Be careful, Mickke D. The bureau does not like to have someone spook a possible suspect. Don't step on any toes or my information channel may dry up."

"No problem, Jim. I'll be careful."

৵৵

I receive the address on my phone, check to see that my .45 is loaded and take my new ride toward Reynoldsburg. I find the computer store in a strip mall off East Main Street, not far from the intersection with Route 256. I drive through the parking lot to see if I notice any surveillance teams. I don't detect anything out of the ordinary, so I park out in the lot at a location where I can easily watch the storefront.

I wait until I see several people enter the store. I figure he won't cause a problem with lots of witnesses. I carefully place my .45 in the concealed holster in the small of my back and walk up to the storefront next door. I slowly walk over to the window of the computer store and peer inside.

There are several people inside talking to a man who probably is the same one Jim told me about. He sort of looks like the guy in the photo. I continue to peer in the window and then suddenly he looks up and sees me watching him. I can tell by the look on his face he is incredibly surprised to see me staring back at him. As soon as he looks back at one of his customers, I disappear from the window and go back to my car. Several minutes later I see him open the front door and step outside. He looks all around and then goes back inside the store.

I have put my plan in motion. He now knows that I know who he is and where he works. He is now on the defense and I'm on the offense. I need to be very careful from now on.

৵৵

While I'm in Columbus, I elect to shake up someone else and call on Von Spineback. I go back to the building where I interviewed Robert Dane, find Marian and ask to see Mr. Spineback. She tells me, after indicating how nice it is to see me so soon, that he is not in, but if I'd leave my card, Mr. Spineback will get back to me. I leave my card, tell her I'll be in touch, and leave the building. I would love to see the look on his face when she gives him my card. I will not hold my breath until he calls me back.

ॐॐ

Stuart Peterson is livid. How in the world did that PI find out who he was and where he worked? How dare he come to his workplace? Stu has always been the intimidating one but now he is being intimidated and he doesn't like it. He wonders if someone leaked the information to the PI and if so, who it was. He knows his third employer did not leak any information, so it has to be one of the Spineback twins or Ginny.

He immediately calls Von Spineback and asks that same question. Von denies any knowledge of a leak from him, Ginny, or Robert Dane. After a while, Stu settles down. He realizes that getting rid of the PI just became a lot tougher. He has to be more careful and calculating.

ॐॐ

One hour later, Von Spineback is also livid. The PI who Stu was supposed to eliminate was just in his office and wanted to talk to him. He must have gone directly from Stu's shop to his office. He calls Stu, tells him the news, and makes it very clear to him that if the guy is not gone soon, he will hire someone else to do the job.

Von's next stop is Robert Dane's office, where he tells Robert to be ready for a possible visit from the annoying PI from Myrtle Beach. He informs Robert not to see him or talk with him but call immediately if he does come around or calls.

Next, he calls Ginny and tells her the same thing. She wants to know what's going on but Von cuts her off, tells her to do as he says, and hangs up.

Chapter 42: Setting a Trap

Once I return to Shaw's, I figure it's time to get ready for all-out war. I'm guessing that between the Spineback twins and Stuart Peterson, someone will be out to get me real soon. I need to work this out so that I pick the place of battle and not my aggressor.

I call big Steve and tell him how my day went and that I'm expecting trouble before very long. I give him all the information I have on the two cases and tell him that I may need his help at some point in time. He tells me that if I had left well enough alone and let the authorities do their jobs, I wouldn't be it this situation. To that statement, I reply, "If I had not opened a can of worms, the authorities would never have reopened either case."

After a slight delay, he responds, "I suppose you're right. Be careful and call me 24/7 if you need help or get in a bind."

Before I hang up, I ask, "Is there an Army/Navy store somewhere in town?"

"Yeah, just south of town where the old Lancaster Sales store was located." He replies with skepticism in his voice. "But they don't sell hand grenades, in case that's what you're looking for."

"Very funny. I'll talk with you later."

Next, I call Jake and give him an update. When I tell him about someone blowing up my car in the parking lot behind Shaw's, he tells me he knew that had to have something to do with me even though the article never mentioned my name. I laugh and teasingly tell him he should have been there, it was more fun than the altercation at Buckeye Lake. Without answering, Jake hangs up.

I drive over to the Army/Navy store to look around. I end up purchasing camouflage pants, a long-sleeve shirt, a floppy hat, some face grease, and some insect repellant. I don't feel right wearing camouflage with tennis shoes but I did not bring my combat boots with me. I also purchase an ammo belt and a hunting knife with a sheath. Next, I stop by a pawn shop and pick up a cheap voice-activated tape recorder as well as a small maglite and a backpack. I wonder what Jake is going to think when he sees these purchases on my expense report.

I go back to Shaw's and try to figure out how I am going to lure my enemies to where I have decided to meet them head on. I can come up with only one plausible location. Mt. Pleasant.

I call Dr. Jon Spineback and Von Spineback. I know I won't be able to get through to them and I am right. Both calls are forwarded to their voice mails. I leave the same message with both. *This is Mickke MacCandlish and I would like to have a face-to-face meeting with you to advise you of what I have discovered about the deaths of Sissy Adams, David Adams, and Sue Ellen North before I go to the authorities. Maybe we can make a deal. I need the meeting to be in a public place, so how about meeting me up on Mt. Pleasant Friday morning at 9:00. Come alone.*

Chapter 43: Beverly Arrives

Beverly Beery arrives in The Bahamas at Andros Town International Airport, located at Fresh Creek. Andros is the largest island in the Bahamas chain. She takes a taxi to the house Liz rented for her. It is a cute, nicely furnished, two-bedroom, two-bath bungalow situated just across the street from the beach and comes complete with a Jeep in the driveway. After getting her things positioned in the house, she arranges her long blond hair in a ponytail, and puts on a ball cap and dark glasses. She locates the keys to the Jeep and heads off to find a consignment shop called Artsy Fartsy Flamingo Bay about two miles away. Liz told her to ask for Lanne Crystal. Lanne appears from behind a curtain. Beverly smiles at her and says, "My name is Cathy Mars. Do you have a package for me?"

She follows Lanne into a back room where she is given a gym bag with the name "Cathy Mars" on it. Beverly thanks her, gathers it up, and leaves the shop. She makes herself a mental note to come back and look around when she has more time. The shop has some neat things in it.

Once in the Jeep, she opens the bag and finds a loaded .9mm handgun and a small .25 caliber revolver, along with three full clips for the .9mm and a box of shells for the smaller weapon. The .25 caliber weapon will fit nicely in her purse or in an ankle holster, which she also finds in the bag. She can wear it when wearing long pants or it will stretch to fit on her thigh if wearing a skirt. In a sealed envelope, she finds $2,500 in cash and a credit card with the name Cathy Mars imprinted on it, along with a driver's license and passport with the same name, and a cell phone. As usual, Liz has thought of everything.

On the way back to her new abode, she stops and makes 500 copies of the 8 X 10 photo Liz gave her of Stephanie. She adds to the photo, "Missing sister – Last Seen Here - $500 reward for info leading to her return – call 843-555-1212." She stops at a local hardware store and purchases a staple gun and a box of staples, along with some heavy- gauge Scotch tape. After leaving the hardware store, she stops by a small local grocery store to purchase some food and a bottle of wine.

She is ready to begin her search but decides to wait until tomorrow. She finds a beach chair in the bungalow, slips the small .25 caliber weapon into her cut-off jeans, along with the envelope with the cash and cards. She puts the gym bag with the .9mm under the bed. She pours herself a glass of wine and walks over to the beach. It's just another beautiful day in paradise. Time to relax before the real work begins. As she relaxes on the beach, she closes her eyes and allows her mind to wander. The sun, the beach, the small beads of sweat beginning to moisten her legs, brings back some good memories. She thinks to herself, *I wonder what Mickke D is doing in Myrtle Beach today.*

She abruptly awakes as a shadow passes over her body. She reaches for her weapon but doesn't complete the move. She takes a deep breath and watches as two young girls pass in front of her, blocking the sun for only an instant. She takes a deep breath and quickly glances at her watch. She sees that she has dozed off for about thirty minutes. She finishes her glass of wine and goes back across the street to the bungalow.

As she walks up the three steps to the porch, she feels a shiver go through her body as she notices a shadowy figure inside the house. She immediately freezes, sits her empty glass on the railing of the porch, and pulls out her weapon. She senses danger.

Chapter 44: TC

TC returns to the Georgetown Library and goes back to work looking at the old coastal maps. He knows exactly where the wreckage of *The Queen Beth* is now located, but he does not know how far she traveled in those two days between the aforementioned burying of the treasure and the demise of the ship. From prior entries in the logbook, he has determined that depending on the wind and currents, she could have traveled anywhere from five to twenty-five miles in that two-day period. So if he backtracks from the ship's current location, it may be anywhere from Murrells Inlet to beyond Georgetown. On the other hand, the ship could have sailed past Murrells Inlet and then turned back toward Pawleys Island. A strong breeze or a powerful storm could have sent her off course. In addition, she could have been lurking in one of the many inlets along the coast waiting for prey. Another possibility is that Captain Swinely may have been looking for a way to abandon ship and leave the crew to fend for themselves. If he was worried about a mutiny, that may have been the best solution. Get off the ship and then return and get the treasure.

TC looks up, his eyes open wide, and thinks to himself, *Oh, my God, what if Captain Swinely didn't die when the ship sank? What if he jumped overboard and swam to safety? What if he scuttled the ship himself and made it look like an attack from pirates?*

TC has a sick feeling in the pit of his stomach. He needs to check and see if he can find out if there's any information on Captain Swinely. He goes up to the front desk at the library and asks the lady if there are any books available on pirates and ship captains from back in the late 1600s to the mid 1700s. She gives him three titles and tells him where they are located. He scans the three books and finds one reference to a Captain Swinely. The reference stated that a Captain Kent Swinely was a revered pirate and supposedly died when his ship sank off the coast of the Carolinas. However, several undocumented accounts from people swore they saw him later in the Bahamas. TC did notice a reference to the remains of a long boat, which was discovered on Goat Island in 1955 in Murrells Inlet. It is believed to be from the early 1700s, which would have been the same time frame as the sinking of *The Queen Beth*. What if Captain Swinely abandoned the ship in a long boat and rowed to Goat Island?

Perplexed and feeling down, he opts to call it quits for the day. He feels it may be time to take a relaxing boat ride and scan the coastline from his boat. Sometimes good things happen when you least expect it.

Penne, at the front desk of the library, makes a note of which three books TC referenced for her friend, the documentary filmmaker.

Chapter 45: Upset Brothers

"**Make a** deal. What is this clown trying to do?" Von Spineback says to no one in particular after listening to his voicemail. He immediately calls Stu and tells him about the voicemail message. He then adds, "Here's your chance, Stuart. Meet this joker on Friday and get rid of him."

Stu knows Von is upset because he used his full name. He tells Von he will take care of the situation. He no sooner hangs up with Von than there is a call from Dr. Jon with the same story. "Stuart, take care of this now! I don't want to hear from this guy ever again."

"No problem, Dr. Jon, consider it done." Stu notices that Dr. Jon also used his full name. Stuart can't figure out why this PI would want to see both brothers on the same day, at the same time, and at the same place. His gut feeling is that it is a trap.

Stuart is going to stand in for Dr. Jon and Von Spineback on Friday but he will be there around 6:30 or 7:00 to be ready for the Myrtle Beach PI. He will have no problem finding his way around because he has been there before, not too long ago. He breaks down his automatic assault rifle, and places it in a carry case along with a silencer. He also cleans his .357 Colt. He calls his other central Ohio client and tells him he may need backup. His client agrees to act as a backup if needed. Stu does not give the person any details on his target. He learned in the CIA that sometimes the less your operatives know, the easier it is to control the operation. Stuart will tell the person where to go, what to do, and when to do it. He hopes his client won't be needed.

Chapter 46: Beverly's Guests

Beverly has two choices: She can go in with gun blazing and ask questions later or walk in as if she does not know someone is there. She goes with the latter. If the person is a common criminal, she can easily overpower him with no problem, but if he is a pro, it may not be as easy.

She puts her weapon in her front pocket with the butt exposed so it will be easy to get to, pulls out her shirt, and covers the gun. She takes a deep breath, unlocks the front door, and walks boldly into the living room as if she is completely unaware of an intruder.

A middle-aged woman in jeans and T-shirt walks out from the kitchen, stares for a second, and then says with an English/Bahamian accent, "Oh, are you the new renter? I was just checking to make sure the place was clean. I didn't know you had already moved in." The woman has a shapely behind, big bust, and shrewd, judgmental dark eyes.

From the corner of her eye, Beverly notices movement and another figure emerges from her bedroom. She turns to see a man, dressed also in jeans and a T-shirt. He also speaks with the same English/Bahamian accent, "Is there a problem, Donna?" He flashes a brilliant and insincere smile but Beverly can see a cloak of impatience all over his face.

Beverly notices a bulge on his left side under his shirt near his waist, which could be a weapon. Smoothly and quickly, she draws her weapon from her pants pocket and points it at the man. "Don't make any quick moves or you will die. You, Donna, move over beside him and both of you put your hands on your heads. Do not speak unless I ask you a question."

Beverly watches as Donna moves slowly toward the man and notices that her nails are well manicured, not the hands of a house cleaner. She also wonders who the lady thinks the stuff in the home belongs to if not her. Looking directly at the woman and with cold-ness and authority in her eyes, she says, "How did you get in here? The front door was locked."

Donna hesitates and then replies, "I have a key to the back door. I told you ...." Beverly puts her finger up to her lips and Donna does not finish her reply. She now turns her attention to the man. "Pull up your shirt slowly with your right hand."

Chapter 47: Plan of Attack

Since I figure whoever shows up Friday morning will be there early, possibly 7:00 or 8:00 to setup an ambush, I am planning to be there by 4:00 or 5:00. I need somewhere to park my car as close to Mt. Pleasant as possible. I don't foresee a lot of traffic at that time of the morning, but a man in full camouflage with a rifle may be a little bit suspicious. I decide to enter Mt. Pleasant from the Fair Avenue side. I remember as a kid there is a back way in from Fair Avenue.

Next, I call Jake. "Jake, do you have any friends who are realtors?"

"Sure, why do you want to know?"

"I need you to find out if there are any houses on Fair Avenue, close to Mt. Pleasant, which are for sale and vacant."

"Please tell me you are not going to break in to someone's house," Jake replies in a begging tone of voice.

"Of course not, just trust me on this one, and I need to know ASAP. And Jake, don't mention my name."

"Your name, damn, I may not mention *my* name."

Jake calls me back in thirty minutes. "There's a house right across the street from the mountain for sale and the realtor said it is vacant and on a lockbox."

"Great, give me the address and I promise I won't break in and get you in any trouble." I write down the address and tell Jake I will keep him advised.

Tomorrow I will do my recon and get everything ready for Friday.

☞☜

The following morning, I have a big breakfast at Shaw's and then head over to Fair Avenue. I find the address Jake gave me and it will work fine. The house sits on the corner of an alley and has a large covered carport in the alley behind the house next to a one-car garage. I can park my car there and no one should notice, particularly at that time of the morning.

I go on down to Maple Street and turn right down the hill. I remember this was always a great sledding hill as a kid. I park on Maple and walk back up the hill to try and find the back entrance to the mountain. About halfway up, I notice a car turning down the hill. The car looks familiar and when the occupant completely ignores me as it passes, I decide big Steve has put a tail on me. He looks like Officer Barrish who brought me the info from the Reynoldsburg detective. That's okay with me as long as he doesn't mess up my plan. It's nice to know he has my back.

I find the partially hidden trail almost directly across the street from Maple, and once I get in the woods I look back down Maple and see the car pull up on the other side of the street and park. Now I'm sure big Steve has put a tail on me. I doubt that he will follow me up the mountain. He probably figures I will return to my vehicle sooner or later.

I pull out a small pad and pencil and make notes as I traverse the trail to the crest of Mt. Pleasant. The trail is very narrow but well defined. Anytime you have a chance to look at terrain in the daytime when you are going to travel that same terrain at night is a good thing. I spend almost an hour previewing the area in and around my ambush location. Once I get back to Shaw's I will go over the entire route and location in my head using my notes.

Now I know where I will enter the trail and how long it will take me to get to the top and my secluded lookout position. The house where I will park is only eight houses down from Maple Street and the beginning of the trail. As I near the trails end on Fair Avenue, I look back down the street and the car that had parked there is still there. As I emerge from the woods, I notice he leaves and turns west onto Lake Street.

I go back to Shaw's and begin to get mentally ready for tomorrow. I go over every step of the way from Fair Avenue to the top of Mt. Pleasant. Next, I pack all of my camouflage clothing and grease in the backpack along with the mosquito repellent, two bottles of water, an energy bar, ammo belt, knife, and recorder. When I leave Shaw's in the wee hours of the morning, I want to look like a person going for an early morning walk, not a soldier on a search and destroy mission.

I test the recorder to make sure it is working. I hope I'll be able to get Stuart or whoever shows up to confess on tape to Sissy's murder.

Now it's time for a power nap. Before I dose off, I picture in my mind my entire trip up the mountain from the time I leave my vehicle until I get to my final destination on the top of Mt. Pleasant. I also go over all entry and exit routes.

I awake ninety minutes later and go downstairs for a nice early dinner. After dinner, I return to my suite, take a nice hot shower, and get in bed by 7:30. I set my alarm for 3:30. I go over the entire plan repeatedly, as I wait for sleep to find its way into my body.

Chapter 48: Beverly's Mistake

Beverly watches closely as the man slowly lifts his shirt and exposes a cell phone in a clip-mounted leather holder. Beverly lowers her weapon to her side and says, "Sorry, I'm a security specialist with Marriott and I am here on a fact-finding mission for the hotel. I get nervous when I find strange people in my house."

"No problem, miss, my husband and I own this home and we were not expecting you until later this evening. We will be leaving now and won't bother you again."

Beverly quickly replies, "Thank you. I would appreciate it if you did not tell anyone I am in town. This is a surprise visit to check on the hotels security awareness. Only the GM knows I'm coming."

"No problem," she states.

Beverly notices a quick glance between the two of them. As the man turns to exit, Donna falls in close to him as they leave the house. Beverly is still just a little bit concerned. She is still holding the weapon in her hand. She saw no cleaning supplies. Maybe they are in the van they are getting into. She walks out behind them, waves, and takes notice of the license number. She will contact Liz and have her run the plate because as the man was leaving and before Donna had a chance to get behind him, she noticed another bulge in the small of his back. It could have been a gun. She decides to call Liz first and ask questions later.

However, on second thought, she races over to the van and again points her weapon at the man's head. She remembers the man coming from her bedroom. If he does have a gun, could it be the .9mm she put under the bed?

"Donna, put both hands on the dash and don't move. You," she says, pointing her weapon at the man's left eye, "get out of the vehicle and put your hands on the van."

As soon as he puts his hands on the vehicle, she pulls up his shirt and sees the .9mm gun she had placed under the bed. She removes the weapon, places it in the small of her back, and tells him to turn around. She now points her weapon at his crotch and says, "You know. I should probably just shoot your sorry ass for stealing my gun. Donna, get out of the vehicle and come over here."

The man's eyes are filled with terror and he is beginning to sweat profusely at the thought of losing some very valuable body parts. Donna comes around the van and stands beside him.

"Now, which one of you is going to tell me what really is going on here?"

Donna raises her hand and speaks, "Okay, the truth is we were watching you from the beach and when we saw you leave the house and come over to the beach, we went over and found the back door open. We were looking for something to steal and sell. We are sorry. We do not mean to cause you any trouble."

Beverly makes a quick decision. "OK, Donna and", looking at the man, "what is your name?"

"Sam."

"OK, Donna and Sam, I have some work that needs done here on the island and if you two are willing to help me, I will not call the police."

"Anything, just name it," Donna replies and Sam nods.

Beverly looks her in the eyes and says, "Do not screw up. I can be a very vengeful person. Do you understand?"

They both nod their heads affirmatively.

She takes them back to the front porch and gets a stack of flyers and the staple gun. Beverly tells them she is actually here to try to find her sister who has been missing for six weeks. She tells them to take the flyers and put them up and pass them out around the island. After they're finished, she tells them to bring the staple gun back and to put it on the porch so she will know they have completed their task. She also tells them that if she goes around the island and does not see any flyers, she will call the police and then she will come looking for them. She makes it very clear to them that if that happens, they had better hope that the police find them before she does.

Donna and Sam thank her and go off on their assigned mission while Beverly goes inside and locks the back door to the house.

As they drive away from Beverly's house, Donna turns and says to Sam, "Mission accomplished."

Chapter 49: Ambush

The alarm clock in my head goes off two minutes before the alarm clock on the nightstand. I turn off the alarm and bounce out of bed. I had a good night's sleep and now it's time to go hunting and see if anyone gets caught up in my snare.

I see no one as I leave Shaw's. The night clerk must have been in the bathroom. The drive over to the mountain is quiet and there is hardly anyone on the streets. I turn off my lights as I turn down the alley and in to the vacant carport in the alley behind the house. I get out of the car and change into my hunting attire. I venture up to Fair and wait until no headlights are visible, and then jog across the street into the tree line. I pause and wait for a few seconds until my eyes become accustomed to the darkness.

I stay in the tree line as I maneuver toward the trail, pausing twice as two cars approach and pass by me on Fair Avenue. I reach the trail and start my journey to the summit. There is a bright crescent moon lurking in the lucid sky, so the trail is easy to follow and there is no need to use my maglite. After an easy ascent, I come off the trail and see the rocky outcrop of the summit. Since I am now in the open with no trees for protection, I carefully and quietly venture forward, my AR-15 at the ready. The sounds and creatures of the night momentarily halt their nightly concerto. The crescent moon is illuminating the rocks, and I stop again to allow my eyes to adjust to the change in light. I slowly frisk the area in front of me with my eyes several times for any movement. I see none.

I reach the top of the mountain where Sissy died and I take time to slowly walk over to the railing and gaze at the twinkling lights of the city below and wonder what it must have been like for her that fateful day.

I quickly return to the present and walk back toward the tree line where I found the Kleenex and the possible location of her waiting killer. I had broken a branch from a tree where I wished to enter when I was up here yesterday and that branch is now visible. I enter the tree line no more than three feet, just far enough not to be seen but not too far back that I can't view a large portion of the rocky pinnacle. I find a tree to rest my backpack and back against and choose a larger tree close by to use as a shield if need be. I settle in for as long as it takes.

The only exposed parts of my body are my face and hands. I smear the camouflage grease on my face and spray repellant on my hands, neck and ears. I can hear the buzz of the mosquitoes but they seem to be shying away from me. Nothing can turn a surprise attack into a disaster as quickly as a swarm of mosquitoes.

My mind wanders back to a night training exercise at Fort Bragg. Twelve of us went out at 2:00 in the morning on a hot and muggy August night. We had to set up an ambush beside a road with tall grass, next to a swamp. It was so bad that the instructors wore mosquito netting over their heads, long sleeves, and gloves. We did not have that luxury. We had to wait for twenty minutes for the convoy to appear that we were to attack. It was absolutely hell, but it was also mind over matter. Ten of us survived but two were sent back to the barracks early. We never saw them again. That was not a fun night.

I have protection now so this should be a walk in the park. I carefully check my watch: and it is 4:15. My eyes have adjusted to the darkness, and with the help of the city lights below I can see the entire rocky top of the summit.

❧❦

Twenty minutes later, just as I am about to reach for a bottle of water, my mouth goes from dry to parched as I hear a branch snap off to my right. My weapon is on my lap pointing left, so I quietly and slowly move my head, shoulders and weapon to the right. At first, I don't see anything, and then about 20 yards away I notice two eyes illuminated by the crescent moon. Just above the eyes, I finally spot the rack of a six-point buck feeding on some tree branches. I remain motionless and the buck, not concerned with me in the least bit, gets his fill and slowly moves away. I am not sure if I have taken a breath in the last five minutes, so I take several deep breaths to slow down my elevated heart rate. I slowly stretch one leg at a time just to keep my legs from going to sleep. I don't need numb legs in case I need to move in a hurry.

Chapter 50: Beverly and Liz

Beverly immediately replaces the Glock under the bed and puts in a call to Liz. Liz returns her call in about five minutes. "Any good news, Beverly?"

"No, not yet. By the way, who did you rent this bungalow from?"

"Well, if you must know, from the lady at Flamingo Bay, Lanne. Why do you ask? Is there a problem?"

"No, I just wanted to know who to call in case I have a problem. Can you check and see if you have anything on a local lady named Donna and her husband Sam?"

"And do you have any last names?" Liz asks.

"Sorry, that's all I've got. I think they're locals; however, their accent has a British twang to it. I caught them in the house and the woman, at first, said she was the owner of the house; however, later they confessed to being thieves after I found out the man had stolen my .9mm from under the bed. I'm trying to figure out if they're just local thieves or what." She gives Liz a detailed description of them and the van they were driving, along with the plate number.

Liz, in a teasing voice, replies, "I hope you didn't torture them. Did you get the gun back?"

"No, and yes I did. Then I put them to work putting up flyers for me around the island."

"Let me see what I can find out. It may take some time since all I have is first names and they may be fake."

The following day, Beverly finds the staple gun on the porch. She drives around town and finds no flyers. She is not a happy camper. Just as she arrives back at her abode, her cell phone rings and Liz's number pops up. "Did you find out anything?" she asks.

Liz replies, "Well, maybe, have you seen anything of Donna and Sam?"

"No I haven't, but they did not do what I asked them to do."

"Be careful, Beverly, I think they may be British Intelligence, and they're looking for Stephanie as well."

"I thought this was *our* case. Why are they involved?"

"Well, sometimes they like to posture themselves and see what they can find out from us. They were probably probing you to find out what you were doing."

Beverly sighs. "Great, and I pretty much told them."

Chapter 51: The Snare Works

It has now been an hour and a half since I arrived and a shaft of early morning sunlight is attempting to split some incoming mist and an emerging fogbank. Before long, the fog may enclose the entire top of the mountain. I may be blinded by the weather. I should have known better. I know to check on upcoming weather before any mission.

All of a sudden, the top of Mt. Pleasant disappears. I can't see more than a foot in front of my face. The early morning has turned quiet. The same quiet happened when I first appeared on the summit. This is not good. Then a whisper of wind seems to blow the fog away. That's when I see him. The outline of a dark figure poised near the railing with what looks like an automatic rifle.

You always think you're ready for any occurrence; however, that is usually not true. Is the fog going to come back? Is he going to move to a point where I can't see him? *Make a decision, Mickke D, you will either be right or wrong.*

I opt not to yell out and startle him. He may just turn and fire. So I say in my normal tone of voice, "That you, Stuart?" hoping he will answer so that I am sure of my target.

Well, so much for that great idea! As he turns, he brings his weapon up and points it in my direction. I instinctively roll to my left as a burst of automatic fire plunges into the tree I was resting against and my backpack dies instantly. I don't believe he saw me or knew where I was located. I'm thinking he fired at the sound of my voice. Another burst of gunfire sprays the area and I'm glad I picked a big tree. He must have a silencer because the sound of the bullets striking the tree is louder than the popping sound of the weapon. I am tempted to put my .45 around the tree and fire off a couple of blind shots, but since the city of Lancaster is right behind him that is probably not a good idea. I need to see my target before discharging my weapon. The firing stops and I sneak a peek around the tree. The fog has come back and my assailant is gone. Where did he go, and why do I have a burning pain in my right side?

Damn, the bastard shot me! When adrenaline is flowing freely, sometimes it takes a while for pain to show up. Well, the pain has arrived, and I can see blood on my shirt. Time to move, I'm a sitting duck here. I retreat but keep the tree between me and the location where I last saw him. About fifty feet back, I blend myself into a large thicket and disappear. I quickly strip off my shirt and T-shirt. I shine my maglite on my side and see where the bullet entered and exited my side. An inch to the right and it would have missed me altogether. An inch to the left and I would be in a world of hurt. I grab my knife and cut the T-shit, ripping it apart with my hands. Next, I take my handkerchief from my back pocket and ball it up. I place the cloth ball on the wound and tie the T-shirt tightly around my waist to hold it in place, putting pressure on the wound. I put my shirt back on and now it's time to move again.

ം⌀ക

Stuart is caught off guard. He once again has underestimated his foe. He is not sure if he wounded or killed Mickke D. He slithers away as the fog moves back in. He begins to sense that curious thrill that comes whenever he finds himself approaching the habitat of his prey. No shots were returned from his opponent, but that doesn't mean he is hurt or dead. He needs to find somewhere to conceal himself and wait to see what happens next.

As he comes off the summit, he opts to head down toward the ledge where he watched Sissy's limp body bounce off and tumble down the mountain. He will set up another ambush and this time do away with this annoying PI. He makes a call on his cell phone, gives some instructions, and hunkers down behind a large boulder, waiting for Mickke D to make the next move. However, he can't wait too long because the sleepy town of Lancaster will awake soon and become a bustling beehive of activity. It's possible a few bird watchers or photographers may even venture up the mountain. The only deterrent right now is the fog.

Chapter 52: Close Call

The fog is not only challenging my sight, but also seems to be deadening sounds around me. The dew on the ground is softening the sounds of my footsteps as well as that of my enemy. I consider calling big Steve, but if he comes up here and Stuart is gone, he will not be a happy camper, so I choose not to make that call right now.

Time is of the essence. My watch reads 6:30 although the fog is disallowing the sun to creep onto the hallowed ground of Mt. Pleasant. Leaving the concealed thicket, I venture slowly back toward the main path, which meanders up the mountain, stopping several times to look and listen, and trying not to get caught out in the open if the fog dissipates.

Upon reaching the path, I decide to venture up toward the summit. I figure he can't see me if I can't see him, but I do stick close to the edge and crouch occasionally to glance around and hopefully hear any non-critter noises. When I reach the point where the concrete steps go up, I decide to go straight, where I was the other day when I found the little-traveled path that dead-ended into the large, forked tree.

It's too damn quiet! I just know Stuart is still here, lurking, waiting for me to make a mistake. Since I am more concerned about looking around instead of down, I accidently step on a branch and the sound of the branch breaking is earth-shattering. The sound no sooner disappears than several shots ricochet off the rocks next to me. It must be Stuart because there are no sounds of gunpowder exploding in the early morning fog.

I quickly move away because he is again firing at sounds. That first move sends a pang of pain through my side and into my brain. I grit my teeth and move on. I have no idea where he is so there's no sense in returning fire. This way he is not sure if it is me or an early morning Mt. Pleasant creature.

I'm beginning to feel as if I'm the only one up here who can't see, because within seconds another volley of shots rings out, except this time I hear the shots and feel the rock chards bang against my legs from the incoming bullets peppering the sandstone ground near my feet. Either Stuart has changed weapons or he has a friend.

I know it is now time to call big Steve, but I also know I can't do it from here. *Move Mickke D, move*, my mind is telling me. I'm just not sure which way to go.

I feel a calm breeze on my face and as quickly as the fog moved in, it just as quickly moves away. I can now see almost thirty yards in every direction. In the fog and fear of battle, decisions are instant and often unconscious. I see the opening to the path leading to the forked tree and I bolt in that direction. Again, pain attacks my brain. I flinch and grab my side as it feels like someone just stuck a knife in my wound. I see a figure to my left; point my weapon and double-tap the trigger, boom-boom. I lose sight of the figure as I jog quickly down the winding path. I can now see the forked tree approaching. I sling the rifle over my back and get ready for a leap of faith. I know this is going to hurt and I have no idea what's on the other side.

Invisible projectiles snap and drop tree branches all around me as I near my last hope, the forked tree. I don't slow down as I put one foot up on the tree and grab with both hands to boost myself up and through the small opening and crash down on the other side.

I was correct; it did hurt. As I survey my surroundings, I am shocked by what I find. My eyes encounter nothing but another big tree, maybe twenty yards away, blocking any chance of escape. The narrow, five-foot path falls off straight down the mountain, and a vine-covered rock cliff encloses the other side.

I hear muted voices coming in my direction. "Where the hell did he go? He couldn't have just disappeared," a voice says that I seem to recognize.

The next voice I hear I have not heard before. "Quiet, just be quiet for a minute. Stay here, I'm going to climb up and look on the other side of this tree. Cover the path; maybe he somehow got behind us, although I don't know how."

"Got you covered. Who is this guy anyway?"

"Keep your eyes open. I'll tell you later," Stuart replies.

My brain is working like a hamster on a wheel. If I see any part of a body appear between the forks of the tree, I will fire. However, if he puts a weapon through and begins firing, I'm in big trouble. There is nowhere to hide.

I lean back against some vines on the rock wall and the vines give with my weight. I reach back with my arm and find open space behind the vines. There must be some type of an opening here. I slowly and quietly remove my knife and quickly cut away enough vines to allow me to squeeze through. I click my maglite to peek around. It's a cave full of skeletons and cobwebs, lending it a mysterious, almost hellish appearance. I can see that the cave disperses into multiple passages, extending like fingers of a hand into the darkness. I feel anxiety, fear, and impending danger here. I want to leave but I can't go back out, at least not yet.

A burst of bullets slam the rock wall and the path, bringing me back to the current problem at hand. Again, the weapon produces no sound.

I hear voices again. "There's nothing over here except another tree. Maybe he fell down the mountain. I'm going over to look around. Be sure to cover the rear."

"Well, hurry, we need to get out of here before anyone shows up."

With my hunting knife in hand, I watch from behind my barrier of vines as a body slowly and carefully clambers down from the fork in the tree. He looks toward the tree blocking the path and gazes over the edge. He turns to face the rock wall and me, concealed behind the vines.

I softly say with my best cloak and dagger voice, "Hey, Stuart, long time, no see." He gazes at the draped curtain of vines with surprised recognition that quickly evolves into anger and fear. Then with surging adrenaline and controlled rage, I attack. I lunge my arm forward through the vines, the long hunting knife blade sliding cleanly into his belly. His eyes open wide as he realizes what is happening. He attempts to raise his weapon but I reach through with my other arm, grab his arm and slice upward while turning my knife, severing his aorta. I feel warm blood on my hand as I remove the knife. He tries to speak but the only thing to come out of his mouth is a trickle of blood. I see naked fear in his eyes, the knowledge that there is no escape, the awareness that he is about to die. Death has raised its ugly face and finally spit on his life. He crumples to the ground in a sea of darkness and rolls over near the edge of the path, gasping for air.

I come out from behind the vines and stare at his limp body trying to find one last gulp of life-giving oxygen. My mind goes instantly to Sissy and Jake. Without a second thought, I take my foot and push him over the edge. I watch as his body tumbles 200 feet below into the trees. I whisper, "That's for Sissy."

戢杣

Back to reality. There's another bad guy on the other side of the tree, not twenty feet away from me. He speaks, "What's going on over there, Stuart, did you find him?"

Before I have a chance to think of a comeback, I hear another recognizable voice, "This is the police. Drop your weapon and put your hands on your head."

"Don't shoot officer, I'm a cop. I was just driving by when I heard shots. I came up here to investigate."

"Do you always investigate with an assault rifle? Drop the weapon now,"

"That you big Steve?" I call out from the other side of the tree.

After a slight pause, Detective Reynolds replies, "Yeah Mickke D, where's the other one?"

The suspect drops his weapon and blurts out, "Mickke D? You have to be shitting me. I should have shot you the other day when you called me Barney."

"The other guy fell off the mountain. The person you have over there is his partner and I'm going to guess his client, Security Guard Fredrick from Pickerington. By the way, is there an EMS unit coming? One of those bastards shot me. I'm going to need some help getting over to your side of this big damn tree."

"Turtle, handcuff this guy, search him for weapons, read him his rights, and then could you please go over and help Mr. Mac-Candlish? I'll call 911."

The adrenaline is receding and the pain is rising in me. I slide down the rocky cliff wall and sit on the path, close my eyes and contemplate my narrow escape. If I were a cat with nine lives, I wonder how many I have left. I am really getting too old for this. I should just retire, buy a big house on the beach and watch all the girls go by and maybe occasionally invite one up for a swim in my infinity pool.

At least the level of frustration and tension I was feeling has decreased and so has the general confusion about the case. It is finally making sense. Now, there is another problem. What form of tormented evil is behind those vines? Where does the cave go, if anywhere? Should I tell anyone about my discovery?

Chapter 53: Now What?

Dr. Jon Spineback tries all day Friday to reach Stuart to no avail. As he is reading the Columbus Saturday morning newspaper, an article on page one catches his attention. The headline reads, "Man Dies on Mt. Pleasant Friday morning in Lancaster."

Dr. Jon smiles. Finally, our PI friend is no longer a threat, he is thinking. However, as he continues reading the article, his smile turns to a frown. The dead man was identified as Stuart Peterson of Columbus. "Son of a bitch," he says to no one in particular.

He calls his wife's name. She is in the laundry room just off the kitchen, "Mary Jo, I think we should take a small vacation. Pack some things and we'll go down to Key West for a while."

"Oh, how romantic Jon. But why not to the Caribbean, maybe Antigua?"

"Sounds great, I'll call Don Scott Field and charter a flight to Key West and we can catch a flight from there to the Caribbean. We'll leave this afternoon."

"Great, I'll call my office and make plans to have someone cover for me. How long do you think we'll be gone?"

"Not sure, just pack light; we can always buy what we need."

Dr. Jon goes to his wall safe, removes every bit of cash, and puts it into a gym bag along with his .38 from the bedroom. He calls his office and leaves a message for his receptionist. He and Mary Jo are going to take a short vacation to Canada for a couple of weeks and could she please call and cancel all of his appointments when she gets in the office on Monday.

∂∾∽

Von Spineback reads the same article. He also could not catch up with Stuart on Friday, and now he knows why. He immediately calls Robert Dane and gives him the news. "If anyone calls you about Stu, you tell them he did some work for us as a computer consultant."

"Sure Von, I understand, but he has always been paid in cash, there is no money trail from us to him."

Von thinks for a minute and then replies, "Good, but I want you to erase any and all calls from us to him or him to us, office phone and cell phones."

"Consider it done and please keep me advised," Robert says in a pleading tone of voice.

Von's next call is to Ginny Ridlinger. "Hey, Stu is dead. Looks like that PI killed him. I hope that he died before anyone had a chance to question him. You need to erase any calls on your cell or office phone from him right away. Was he ever in your office?"

Ginny pauses before answering, trying to digest what Von has just bestowed upon her. "No, the only time I was ever with him was when we were all up at Buckeye Lake for lunch that day. What are we going to do?"

"For now, we are not going to do anything. Just go on as if nothing has happened and if you are questioned, just dummy up. They can't prove anything."

Chapter 54: The Hospital

I remember Officer Barrish helping me over to the other side of the tree but that was about it until I woke up in the emergency room at Lancaster Hospital. The doctors told me they gave me some blood and did surgery to clean up and sew up my gunshot wound. They told me that my makeshift bandage saved my life. The bullet had nicked a couple of blood vessels and I had lost a lot of blood. They told me I was a lucky guy. They advised me to take it easy for a while and put me in a recovery room. They decided to keep me overnight and release me tomorrow. I agree because I am too tired to disagree.

I no more than get to my room and close my eyes when big Steve barges in. "So Mickke D, tell me what happened. I would really like to hear the part about the guy falling off the mountain."

I try to sound as sick as possible. "Aren't you supposed to knock before coming in here? The doctors and nurses do."

"Yes, but they don't know you as well as I do."

I continue, "And while I'm thinking about it, could you please call Donna Crist and tell her it's OK to come home?"

"Sure." Before he has a chance to interrogate me, the door opens again and in walks Jake.

"Jake, what the hell are you doing here? Damn, I thought I was here to get some rest. I was shot. I just had surgery. This room is a revolving door of chaotic intrusions."

"Hey, big Steve called and said you had been shot. I rushed over to check on you."

Detective Reynolds turns and sneers at Jake. Jake, remembering what I had told him about big Steve's promise to deck us if we called him big Steve, clears his throat and says with a sly grin, "I mean Detective Reynolds called."

Still sneering, Detective Reynolds replies, "Thank you Jake, now sit down and shut up while I talk to our friend here," as he turns back to look at me.

Those were the last words I remember hearing. I guess whatever the nurse gave me finally kicked in and I was off in La-La land dreaming about my big house on the beach and girls in bikinis around my infinity pool.

Chapter 55: Beverly and Rick

The day after Beverly finds out Donna and Sam did not pass out her flyers, she goes out and does the job herself, placing flyers on telephone poles, buildings, and in businesses. She keeps a close eye out for any tails, but she notices no one. She calls Liz and tells her she is going on down to Puerto Rico and the Virgin Islands next. Liz tells her she will have Lanne keep an eye on the house while she's away. She also gives her the name and number of a pilot she can trust who can fly her to her destinations while she's there.

"Does he work for us?" Beverly asks.

"Well, sort of," she replies. "One might say he's a paid consultant and if you need backup, he's available. You can trust him. Tell him GG gave you his number."

"GG? Where did that come from?"

"From my granddaughter. When I'm in a bad mood, she calls me grumpy granny." She curtly replies.

"Thanks Liz, I'll give him a call."

"He will probably want you to pay him up front, but, tell him to bill me. He knows the rules." Before she ends the call, Liz says, "Be careful and keep me advised."

Beverly calls the number Liz gave her and asks for Rick. "This is Rick, what can I do you out of?"

Beverly pauses. "I need some transportation. GG gave me your number."

After a slight hesitation, he replies, "Ah yes, GG. I take it you need to hire a pilot."

"Yes, I would like to make a stop in Puerto Rico, the Virgin Islands, and maybe a few other places. Can we leave tomorrow?"

"Sure thing darlin', I'm based out of San Andros Airport. What time do you want to leave and how do you want to pay for this?"

"How about 9:00 in the morning and don't give me any shit. You know to bill….GG." She almost slipped and said Liz.

"Sorry, can't blame a guy for trying to get paid up front. And what do I call you?"

She ponders the question, smiles to herself, and then answers, "Scarey Mary, which means I'm a real mean bitch."

"OK, why don't I call you MB for mean bitch. I see we're going to get along just fine," he quirks, "see you at 9:00, Hanger B-2."

Beverly goes out and makes more copies of her flyers to take with her on the flight. She then goes back to the beach for a little relaxation before going to work.

Chapter 56: The Interview

Tuesday morning, I meet big Steve for breakfast at Shaw's. After some small talk, he tells me that Officer Fredrick pretty much clammed up and wanted an attorney. After doing some background work, the police found that Fredrick was retired Coast Guard and had come into a large inheritance. They also discovered that about five years ago, Officer Fredrick lost some good friends to a drive-by drug shooting, seemed to lose it, and vowed to eliminate the drug problem himself. That was about the period when several drug-related murders began. No one seemed to care much because the victims were either drug dealers, pimps, or addicts. They found several cell phone calls from Frederick to Stuart Peterson's computer shop in Reynoldsburg, which coincided with some of the murders. They did find Stuart's cell phone; however, the calls were encrypted, and since the phone manufacturer denied them a backdoor because of privacy issues, they could not download any information from his phone. Therefore, they could tie Fredrick to Stuart but not Stuart to anyone else. He also told me he should have a warrant to search Mr. Peterson's computer business within the next couple of days. He hopes they'll find something there.

Now it was my turn in the barrel. "So, Mickke D, tell me about how Mr. Peterson fell off the mountain."

I do not hesitate with my answer, "It's actually pretty simple. He came over, we got into a fight, I won, and he fell off the mountain. End of story. And by the way, why were you up there Friday morning?" I ask, trying to change the subject.

He raises his eyebrows and says, "I had a tail on you and I was up there saving your sorry ass. Do you have a problem with that?"

"Not at all. I knew you had a tail on me."

With a scoffing look, he replies, "Whatever, let me ask you this. He was stabbed, not shot. Why didn't you just shoot him?"

"Detective, did you see how narrow that path was on the other side of that tree? There wasn't room for his rifle and my rifle. I quickly decided that a knife would be a better weapon and I was right."

I figure from his question that he was not on the other side of the forked tree. I guess that means neither he nor Officer Barrish found the vine-covered cave entrance.

"Mickke D, you never cease to amaze me. So tell me why all of you were up on Mt. Pleasant Friday morning?"

After a sip of honey-laced hot green tea, I reply, "Well, I had pretty much decided that somehow Dr. Jon Spineback was involved with the death of Sissy's husband and the later death of Sue Ellen North. I also thought that his twin brother Von Spineback was somehow involved in Sissy's death. Therefore, I called both of them and told them to meet me on Mt. Pleasant Friday morning or I was going to the police. I arrived early to see who was going to show up. It was Stuart and later Officer Fredrick. I also believe Stuart probably killed Sissy, Kevin and tried to kill Donna Crist as well. Oh, and by the way, one of them shot me. I presumed I had a right to defend myself."

"Well, the only problem is that we have no way to tie Stuart to either Jon or Von Spineback and less evidence to tie Stuart to Sissy's death, Kevin's death and Donna Crist's attempted murder. Do you have any ideas?"

I hesitate and then reply, "Yes I do. I have a photo of Von Spineback with Stuart and Ginny Ridlinger up at Buckeye Lake."

"OK, so how do you know it was Von and not Jon and who the hell is Ginny Ridlinger?"

"Well, for the answer to your second question, Ginny is the director of public relations at Anchor Hocking and I think she is having an affair with Von. They were both in the Air Force at the same time, although I can't place them serving together anywhere. Maybe you can find that out. I also think that somehow Anchor Hocking is right in the middle of it all. And that hopefully answers question number one."

"OK, let me see the photo."

I pull up the photo on my phone and show it to him. "There, is that proof enough?"

"Nice picture of three people but, not a close-up. It won't stand up in court. Could be Jon, could be Von, and the woman's face is hard to see. You should have got closer to them."

"Well, detective, I didn't want them to know I had seen them together." I then ask, "So why don't you bring them in and ask some questions? Maybe one of them will crack."

"Maybe I will, Mickke D, maybe I will. Email me that photo."

He hesitates and then asks, "So when are you going back to the beach?"

"Well, I'm not sure. I go back to the doctor tomorrow and I'll see what he says."

"OK, but before you leave, I need you to come down to the station and give a deposition about what happened on Mt. Pleasant, just in case we need you to testify at some point." He gets up and says, "Got to go, take care of breakfast, you owe me."

Before I have a chance to counter, he turns, raises his hand, and leaves the restaurant.

Chapter 57: Rick

Beverly brings both weapons and her stash of money with her to the airport to meet Rick. She learned her lesson about leaving anything valuable at the house.

As she enters the hanger, a guy with a big grin on his face walks up and says, "What do you have in the bag, MB? It looks heavy."

"You must be Rick. Hey, did I ask you what you had for breakfast?" she curtly replies.

She sizes Rick up. He is not a very big guy, sort of looks like Jimmy Buffet, and he has had a grin on his face since he first walked up to her. However, she can tell from his hardened gray eyes that he has clearly witnessed the darker side of life. She sees him as sort of a dashing figure with just a hint of snake oil. She tells herself to stay alert and be careful. She just knows Rick is going to tax her patience level.

They walk out on the tarmac to his plane and she remarks, "Nice ride, Rick, what is it?"

"That young lady is a 421 Cessna, a pressurized twin piston with a cruising speed of 240 mph. It has a range of anywhere from 810 miles to a max of 1,400. She'll seat six plus a crew of two. She is a great island-hopping plane. Are you ready?"

"I'm ready, how long will it take us to get to Puerto Rico?"

"Let me worry about that. Are you sitting in the back or upfront with me?"

"I'll sit up front." She takes a seat in the co-pilot's seat and buckles up.

Rick sits down in the pilot's seat and remarks, "By the way, it's about 840 miles. We should be there between 12:30 and 1:00. You can buy lunch."

ॐॐ

Inside the small airport complex, Donna and Sam watch as Rick and Beverly cruise down the runway and take off into the wild blue yonder.

෨෴

There is not a lot of conversation on the trip. Beverly dozes and Rick puts the plane on autopilot and reads a book.

She wakes up and checks her watch. It's 10:30. Rick is still reading his book. "What are you reading?" she asks between yawns.

"It's called 'Cougars at the Beach' and it takes place in Myrtle Beach, South Carolina. Met a guy in Colombia who lives up there. He said it's a cool place. I've been thinking about taking a trip up there to look at a bar I found for sale on the internet. Would you believe it, it's called Ricky's Dockside Bar & Grill? I won't even have to change the name or buy a new sign."

Beverly's heart ends up in her throat. She can hardly speak. "Sounds great. I've never been to Myrtle Beach but I've heard good things about it." She closes her eyes and lets her mind drift, hoping Rick will go back to reading.

"I only have a few chapters to go. I'll let you read it when I'm finished."

"That's all right, I'm not much of a reader." She turns her head away from him, discreetly brushes a tear from her cheek and dozes off again.

Chapter 58: Big Steve & Ginny

Detective Reynolds walks into Anchor Hocking's offices on West Fair Avenue, flashes his badge, and asks to see Ginny Ridlinger. Ginny appears within seconds and extends her hand. Steve takes note of the firm handshake and asks her, "Could we talk in private, Ms. Ridlinger?"

"Why of course Detective, come into my office." *Said the spider to the fly*, Steve thinks.

"Ms. Ridlinger, do you know a man by the name of Stuart Peterson?"

"Let me think, Stuart Peterson. That name does ring a bell. There was a Mr. Peterson who did some computer work for us a while back, but I don't really remember his first name. Why do you ask?"

"Well, he was killed on Mt. Pleasant Friday morning and your name has come up in the investigation. I just need to eliminate you as a possible suspect."

"Suspect? I was here at work Friday morning at 7:45. How could I be a suspect?" He can tell by the tone of her voice she is beginning to become upset. He does not want to spook her and have her ask for an attorney.

"Oh, it's probably nothing, Ms. Ridlinger, but I have a photo of someone who I think is you, taken at Buckeye Lake with two gentlemen and I think one of them is Stuart Peterson." He shows her a copy of the photo Mickke D emailed him.

He notices her face turning a slight shade of pink and then she regains her cool. "Well detective, I don't know who that woman is, but it's not me. I'm fairly new in town and I have never heard of Buckeye Lake."

"So you don't recognize the other man as Von Spineback, president of Wilmont Oil & Gas?"

She answers immediately, "Sorry, never heard of a Von Spineback or Wilmont Oil & Gas. Anything else I can help you with, detective. I do have work to do here."

"No, I think that's about it. Thanks for seeing me, Ms. Ridlinger. "So, you never met a Von Spineback while you were in the Air Force?"

"I was in the Air Force, but I don't remember meeting a Von Spineback."

"OK. Thanks. I'll give you a call if I think of anything else."

"Anytime." She sees him to the door and closes it once he has left the office. She takes a deep breath, goes to her desk, and calls Von Spineback.

"Von, the police were just here and they have a picture of you, me, and Stuart at Buckeye Lake. He also asked if I had met you in the Air Force. Now, what do we do?"

Von hesitates before replying, "And what did you tell them?"

"I told them the girl in the picture wasn't me and that I did not know you. I said a Mr. Peterson had done some computer work for us."

"Good girl, That's our story and we'll stick with it. Stu is dead so they can't question him. If they ask me, I'll say I took Stuart to lunch one day and he brought his girlfriend along but I don't know you and you don't know me. Be sure and delete this call from your phone and don't call me again, I'll call you. Oh yeah, one more thing. Get yourself a haircut. I don't want you looking anything like the girl in the photo."

Once Detective Reynolds gets to his vehicle, he calls Von Spineback. His plan is to ask him in a polite way to come down to Lancaster and answer a few questions about the death of Stuart Peterson. Von's secretary says he is on another call, can he hold? *I'll just bet he is,* he is thinking to himself. "Yes, I can hold, thank you."

Within seconds, Von answers the call and Detective Reynolds poses the question to him. "Should I bring my attorney? What is this about? What does Stuart Peterson's death have to do with me?" he asks.

"I don't know Mr. Spineback, do you need an attorney? Have you done anything wrong?" His polite tone of voice turns into an authoritative attitude.

"Well, in my business, someone is always suing me, just asking," Von replies.

"Sorry about that Mr. Spineback. I'll see you tomorrow morning at 11:00."

His next call is to Dr. Jon Spineback's office and he is told by Dr. Jon's secretary that he and his wife went on a vacation to Canada. They are not expected back for two weeks. He leaves his name and number with the secretary and asks her to have him call as soon as he returns.

He then calls the Columbus International Airport to see if Dr. Jon or his wife booked a flight. Neither name shows up on their computers.

Chapter 59: Beverly's Plan

Beverly and Rick land in Puerto Rico at 12:30. As they leave the plane, Rick hands Beverly the book he was reading. She looks him straight in the eyes, "I told you I'm not a reader, you can keep your damn book."

He quickly pulls the book back. "No problem, MB, what's on our agenda?"

Beverly regains her composure. "We're going to grab a quick sandwich, then you're going one way and I'm going the other way and we're going to put up and pass out flyers. Where can we rent a couple of cars?"

They grab a bite to eat. Ricky finds a place to rent two cars for a couple of hours and they each pass out about 50 flyers. They meet back at the plane at 3:00.

"How long will it take us to get to The Virgin Islands?" she asks.

"Not long, it's only about 110 miles from here to there," Rick replies. "We'll fly into the Cynil E. King Airport on the western end of St. Thomas. Are we doing the same thing there?"

"Yes, we are. I'd like to get flyers out today. We'll spend the night there and then fly on down to Antigua and Barbados tomorrow. I figure we can spend the night in Barbados and then fly back to the Bahamas the next day."

"Works for me, since GG is footing the bill."

Beverly sits in the back of the plane on the trip to The Virgin Islands. She doesn't want to hear anymore about Rick's book or Myrtle Beach. They get their work done and she rents two rooms at Secret Harbour Beach Resort on St. Thomas. They have an early breakfast and are on their way to Antigua by 8:00 the next morning. She moves back up to the co-pilot's seat. She has to ask Rick one question. "So who was this guy you met in Colombia from Myrtle Beach?"

Rick turns, surprised she is talking to him. "His name was Mickke D, never knew his last name. He was ex-Special Forces."

"And what were you guys doing in Colombia?"

"Sorry darlin', that's classified. I probably already said too much. You and I both know there are some things one does not discuss."

"Absolutely." she replies as she takes a deep breath to calm her heart rate.

It's a short flight to Antigua. She tries to sleep but that never happens. They do their thing with the flyers, grab a sandwich at a deli just off the beach, and take off for Barbados by 1:30. They arrive shortly thereafter at Grandtey Adams International Airport in Barbados. Beverly calls and reserves two rooms at the Dover Beach Hotel in Bridgetown, they rent a couple of cars and do their thing with the flyers. By 5:00, they are finished. Beverly figures they have passed out more than 500 flyers so far.

Beverly's phone starts ringing constantly. The possibility of a fast $500 brings out a hoard of possible sightings. She always asks three questions when she receives a call. What does she look like? Where did they see her? What is the caller's name? If they don't mention the fact that she was almost 5'10" tall, she just thanks them and says she'll get back to them.

Chapter 60: Stephanie's Surprise

Stephanie Langchester takes a break from the beach and decides to grab a sandwich and a glass of wine at The Deli, which is located just off the beach in Antigua. She takes one step into the open front door and hastily retreats back outside. She can't believe her eyes. Sitting at a table in The Deli is a girl who looks exactly like Mickke D's girlfriend back in Myrtle Beach.

She purchases a paper and sits down at an outside table. From behind the paper, she watches as the girl she believes to be Beverly and someone else leave the restaurant. She is thinking to herself, *why would she be here and who is she with?*

After they leave, she ventures back inside the deli but again makes a hasty retreat. She sees a poster or flyer with her picture on it lying on a table next to the register. Someone is looking for her lost sister, no name, just a reward and a phone number. She puts on her sunglasses and hat, goes back in with her newspaper covering part of her face, picks up the flyer, and leaves.

Stephanie figures British Intelligence is looking for her, but what is the connection between Beverly being here with a stranger and the flyer turning up at the same time. She hurries out to the street and looks both ways to try to see which way they went. She catches a glimpse of them about a block away and moves quickly to get closer.

She watches as Beverly and her friend stop at a corner, waiting for the light to change before crossing the street. She quickly dials the number on the flyer and watches as Beverly reaches into her purse and answers her phone. "This is Mary." The voice belongs to Beverly. She remembers it well from the night they met at TC's.

Chapter 61: Back to the Beach

Good news abounds today. My doctor tells me I am good to travel but not to do anything strenuous for a few weeks. My insurance agent calls and tells me I can pick up a new SRX at the Cadillac dealership in Lancaster and that I can leave my rental car there. I call Jake and tell him to meet me for dinner at Shaw's and that I will be heading back to the beach tomorrow morning. I call Jim and TC to let them know I am on my way home. Jim reminds me about the OSU shirts, so I make a trip to the mall on the way to pick up my new SRX. On the way back, I stop by The Ohio Glass Museum and do a tour. What a neat place, lots of history and even an on-site glass blower. My last stop is at the police station. I give my deposition and make sure big Steve returned my borrowed automatic rifle. I leave a note on his desk stating he has a rain check for dinner.

❧

There's not a lot of chatter at dinner, but while we're having coffee Jake says, "Mickke D, I really want to thank you for what you did. I know Sissy would thank you also."

"No problem, Jake, I was happy to help." I was not going to tell Jake about the cave but at the last minute, I change my mind. "Jake, I've got something else to tell you, but you need to promise me you won't say a word to anyone else."

"No problem, what's going on?"

I hesitate. "Jake, when I was up on the mountain Friday, I found a cave and finding that cave saved my life."

"What are you talking about, what cave?"

I go over the entire story with him and then say, "Jake, you need to promise me you won't go up there until I come back in the fall. We'll go up together. I don't know where it goes but there was something evil about it. I think I was more afraid of it than Stuart Peterson."

"I can't believe you found a cave. No problem, you have my word. I'll wait till you come back." He raises his hand and we high-five. I tell him I'll send him a bill and he thanks me again. I leave bright and early the next morning for Myrtle Beach.

Chapter 62: Von's Interrogation

Von Spineback arrives on time to meet with Detective Reynolds and he does not bring his attorney.

Detective Reynolds does not beat around the bush. He shows him the picture Mickke D took at Buckeye Lake. "Is that you, Mr. Spineback?"

Without missing a beat, he answers, "Why, yes it is. Mr. Peterson did some computer work for me and I invited him for a boat ride in my antique speedboat and then lunch. He brought his girlfriend along. I think her name was Betty something."

"So the girl in the picture is not Ginny Ridlinger from Anchor Hocking?"

"Sorry detective, I don't know a Ginny Ridlinger."

"Are you sure, Mr. Spineback? I thought you two served in the Air Force together?"

He wavers for just a second and then replies, "Detective, I met a lot of women in the Air Force, but that name does not ring a bell."

Detective Reynolds can tell Von has rehearsed all of his answers, so he adds one last question. "Did you know that Mr. Peterson was also working for your brother Jon?"

Von stares back at him with contempt in his eyes, eyes that are not sad or mournful, but cold and almost angry. "Detective, if my brother had a computer problem, I guess that could be a real possibility. Anything else?"

"No, Mr. Spineback, that's all for now. However, if you decide to leave town, please notify me. Your brother left town on Saturday, do you have any idea where he might have gone?"

Von stands up and heads toward the door. He stops, turns, and replies, "Detective, I am not my brother's keeper. Never have been, never will be."

As soon as Von reaches his car, he calls Ginny, "We need to be extra careful. They know we were both in the Air Force at the same time but they can't prove any relationship. I told them the girl in the photo was Stu's girlfriend. We need to try and speed up the sale if at all possible. Don't call me, I'll call you. Delete this call."

He hangs up without Ginny being able to get a word in edgewise. She just shakes her head and deletes the call.

ತಿ∘ನ

Ginny is having second thoughts about this whole situation, the hook-up with Von and the sale of the distribution center. She begins making plans of her own, that do not include Von. She is thinking that she has a girlfriend from the Air Force who manages a bar in Antigua. She's been conversing with her on Face Book. Maybe she will quit her job, disappear for a while, surprise her girlfriend and spend some time with her. The only thing she will lose is her job and she still has her retirement from the Air Force. She's renting a furnished apartment on a month-to-month basis and her SUV is paid for. Her retirement is not a lot, however, it will keep her solvent.

Now the question is, does she blow the whistle on Von before she leaves? Although he never came right out and told her, she is sure he had the reporter killed on Mt. Pleasant because she was getting close to figuring out what he was about to do. In addition, she knows for sure he sent Stu after Mickke D. So if that's the case, will he try to get rid of her, as well?

Chapter 63: Mr. Plum

After talking with Mickke D, TC does some calculations and figures it will take them almost 86 hours, island-hopping by boat, to get to Antigua. That would be in calm seas and the total days to get there would be five or six. He decides to check into flying there and then renting a boat and dive equipment to check out the salvage site.

He made his boat trip down the coastline and found nothing that looked positive to him. He has pretty much convinced himself that they will never find the location of Captain Kent Swinely's buried treasure, if there actually is buried treasure, so the salvage trip will be a good distraction. Maybe afterward, he and Mickke D can come back and start out with a fresh prospective.

Since money is not an issue, he books a Lear Jet from Jet Express in Myrtle Beach to fly them to Antigua. The departure date is three days after Mickke D returns to the beach. He figures he will be ready for a vacation. He calls his contact in Antigua and tells him to expect them Thursday. His contact tells TC he will rent two rooms at the Carlisle Bay Antigua for them. He asks his contact to see about renting them a boat and some dive equipment to check out the salvage site. His contact assures him his request will be taken care of.

TC has never met his contact. A Mr. Plum contacted him and said he had read about his discovery off the coast of South Carolina and that he had a site off the coast of Antigua that he would like searched. He said he would pay him $25,000 up front toward his expenses and if they found any treasure, TC would receive 25% of the proceeds. The whole thing sounded like a new paid adventure to TC, and after Mickke D said he would come along, TC agreed.

TC should have looked closely into his contact. Mr. Plum is the leader of a Colombian hit team, set up by the son and family of

Pablo Valdez, the cartel drug lord who Mickke D killed in Colombia. The son and family have vowed to eliminate Mickke D. They did their homework and they know that Mickke D is partners with TC. They decided to get them off the mainland and out of their comfortable environment with a ruse.

The Colombian hit team consists of three cartel members who are loyal to the late Pablo Valdez and his family. Mr. Plum is the fourth member and the person in charge. He arranged to get TC and Mickke D to Antigua. So far, the plan is working and now they know when they are arriving, where they are staying, and that they need a boat and dive equipment. They now have two days to plan their attack. They could hit them where they are staying, on the boat, tamper with the dive equipment or just walk into a restaurant where they are eating and kill them. The family could care less. They just want Mickke D gone from the face of the earth. The choice belongs to them.

Chapter 64: Back "At the Beach"

My trip back to the beach is uneventful. I do make several stops to walk around and to keep an eye on my wound. It seems to make the trip without any complications.

I hear Blue growling as I unlock my door, however, when he sees me, he goes crazy and starts jumping up on me as I try to protect my wound. After he calms down, and a trip outside for him to pee, I call Jim and tell him I'm home. He says welcome back and that he saw me pull in. I tell him to come over and get his OSU stuff.

We discuss my Ohio adventure and what has been going on at the office. He helps me get the SUV unloaded and then after he leaves, I call TC. "Hey TC, I'm back. What are our plans? I'm ready for some R & R."

"We leave Thursday and we're flying instead of taking the boat. We'll rent a boat and gear when we get there."

"Sounds great since it's your nickel."

"Meet me at Jet Express at the airport Thursday morning at 8:30. We depart at 9:00. Pack for about two weeks."

"So, private jet, two weeks in the Caribbean, sounds great to me, can't wait! See you then."

I spend the following two days getting everything caught up at the office and everyone did a great job, no problems. When I tell them I am leaving again to go to the Caribbean, they all question my rush to leave town. My answer is I need a vacation. I pack light and since we're flying a private jet, I include my .45 and three extra clips, just in case we run into pirates.

Chapter 65: Ginny's Plan

Ginny has decided on a plan of action. She will tell her boss she is going to take a much-needed two-week vacation but not where she is going. This way, Von won't find out where she went and she will still get paid. Her checks will be deposited in her bank account. If she decides to come back, everything will be fine. If she decides to stay, everything will be fine as well. She will have her funds transferred to wherever she ends up. She will take most of her personal stuff with her, just in case she doesn't come back.

As far as blowing the whistle on Von, she figures he will probably hang himself. Without her to speed up the sale of the distribution center, things will move at a snail's pace and Von will grow impatient not knowing where she is or if she has ratted him out to the police. He will have no one on the inside at Anchor Hocking, and without Stu there will be no one to do his dirty work. She figures he will probably self-destruct.

Ginny makes the decision. She marches off to her boss's office and gives him the news. Her boss tells her to go and have fun wherever she ends up going. She books the first flight she can find to Antigua.

She leaves Columbus International Airport the following morning at 10:30. Von calls her at 11:00. She does not answer her cell phone. Von then calls her office and her secretary tells him she went on a two-week vacation. He is speechless, "What do you mean a two-week vacation? I need to speak with her right now!"

❧❦

Von Spineback is livid. He can't figure out where Ginny could have gone and why she won't answer her cell phone. He can see everything he has worked for going down the tubes. Without

Ginny, his shell company, which cost him a bunch of money to set up, will have a more difficult time getting the sale of the distribution center through the sales and permit process. Without the distribution center, the rail spur, and the natural gas pipeline, his cost to produce his discovery will increase ten-fold and the price of oil is already heading south. In addition, without Stu he has no enforcer and no way to get computer information on the people he may want to bribe to get the whole thing done. And speaking of Stu, why was he working for his brother? And, last but not least, did Ginny or Stu leave any type of a trail that would lead back to him?

∂∾⊸

Detective Reynolds calls her office that afternoon with some more questions and receives the same message as Von. The difference is that Detective Reynolds can find out where she went and he does. So now, Dr. Jon Spineback and his wife have left the country and so has Ginny Ridlinger. He immediately puts a tail on Von Spineback. He doesn't want all of his chickens to fly the coop.

Chapter 66: Trip to Antigua

I arrive at the Jet Express hanger early, at 8:15. I don't want to be late for this trip. TC arrives about ten minutes later and I fill him in on my Ohio trip. He doesn't say *I told you so,* he just shakes his head.

Just as we are about to climb the stairs to board the plane, my phone rings. It's big Steve. "Thought I would let you know what's going on up here. We finally got a warrant to search Stuart Peterson's computer shop and apartment today. Dr. Jon and his wife left the country and I just found out yesterday that Ginny Ridlinger is on her way to Antigua."

I stop dead in my tracks. I don't know what to say. "You have got to be kidding me! That's exactly where I'm headed."

"Where, out of the country or Antigua?" he replies.

"Both, TC and I are on our way to Antigua for a salvage recon."

"Well, if you see Ms. Ridlinger, tell her I have some more questions for her."

I resume my trip up the stairs, then stop, and say, "What about Von Spineback, did you lose him also?"

"No, smart ass, I put a tail on him right away. Let me know if you run into Ms. Ridlinger." He ends the call abruptly.

I was trying my best to forget about Ohio, but here we go again. Why would Ginny Ridlinger be going to Antigua, why did Dr. Jon Spineback leave the country, and where did he go?

સ્જ

Mr. Plum is waiting for us at the airport. He is wearing a white, tieless suit, a Panama hat and is chewing on a cigar. He has a thick Latin accent. "Judge Cadium, I presume, how nice to meet you. I take it this is your partner?"

"Yes, Mr. Plum, this is Mr. MacCandlish."

He extends his hand and with a wimpy-like handshake, he says, "Nice to meet you, Mickke D."

I gaze at him with inquisitive eyes, "Why did you refer to me as Mickke D, Mr. Plum?" I have pretty much decided I do not like this person. He looks like he just came out of an old Humphrey Bogart movie.

With a perplexed look on his face, he replies, "Oh, I guess Judge Cadium must have mentioned your name at some point in our conversation. Anyway, I hope you don't mind getting your $25,000 in cash." He pats a briefcase he is holding and hands it to TC. "My people do not like to leave a money trail when it comes to salvage rights."

TC looks at me and then turns back to Mr. Plum. "We have no problem with cash."

"Great, here are the keys to your rooms at The Carlisle and I have a rental car waiting outside for you. I'll pick you up tomorrow morning at 10:00 at the Carlisle and take you to the boat. You can look it over along with the dive equipment."

We shake hands with Mr. Plum and watch as he leaves the terminal. TC lays the briefcase on a small end table and asks, "Should we count it?"

"Absolutely not. Do not open that briefcase. What do you know about this Mr. Plum?"

"Well, not much, he told me he read about our salvage of *The Queen Beth* and wanted us to look into a possible location of a wreck off the coast of Antigua. He said he would give us $25,000 up front and 25% of what we find."

"Did you ever mention my name to him and did you notice that cigar he was chomping on?"

"Well, I guess I could have mentioned your name. What has his cigar got to do with anything?"

"That cigar, my friend, if my memory serves me right, is only manufactured in Bogota, Colombia, and is meant for chewing, not smoking. One of the Colombian soldiers I worked with used to chew on one all the time."

"And what does that have to do with our money?"

I look him straight in the eyes. "That soldier came to the States and tried to kill me."

Chapter 67: The Salvage Trip

TC and I take the briefcase with us and put it in the trunk of our rental car. I guess I'm becoming paranoid, because I get down on my hands and knees and look under the car and even open the hood and look inside. I get some strange looks from not only TC but also everyone standing around outside the car rental terminal.

Once we get to TC's room, I check the briefcase over for any wires and listen for any ticking from inside. TC thinks I am absolutely nuts. I unsnap each lock separately and listen for any inside noises. I ask TC to back away and I use a coat hanger to open the case. Nothing blows up or catches on fire. We find no explosives inside, and after counting, all $25,000 in cash is there. Maybe I am becoming paranoid.

Since there are no safes in our rooms, I suggest TC take the briefcase down to the front desk and have them keep it in their office safe. Before doing that, he takes $1,000 from the case for walking around money and puts it in his fanny pack. We spend the rest of the day just lounging around the hotel and talking about our soon-to-be salvage adventure, or at least TC does. I keep searching the area for any possible assassins and wondering if Ginny Ridlinger is going to walk in the front door.

We meet Mr. Plum at 10:00 the following morning, and he is wearing the same clothes and hat he was wearing yesterday and he has a cigar sticking out of his lapel pocket. I sit up front with him and TC gets in the back. As soon as we get moving, I ask, "Where do you get your cigars, Mr. Plum?"

Before he can answer, I hear TC whisper under his breath, "Here we go."

"I buy them from a store here in Antigua, why do you ask?"

"Well, a friend of mine used to chew on them back in Colombia and he always said that was the only place you could purchase them."

Sounding somewhat irritated, he replies, "Well, I guess they decided to branch out and market them all over."

I opt to shut up about the cigars and pay more attention to where we are going. We arrive at the marina about 10:30 and Mr. Plum walks us over to the boat he has rented for us. I notice several not-so-savory looking characters in the general vicinity and I touch my holstered .45 in the small of my back just to give me that warm and fuzzy feeling. They all smile at us and go on with whatever they are doing.

Spread out on the dock is all of the dive equipment TC had told Mr. Plum we needed. We test all of the cylinders and go over each piece of equipment. Everything seems first class and certified. The boat itself is rather dated, but it looks seaworthy and it will work fine for what we will be doing.

"Here are the keys to the boat. There's a cooler on board with sandwiches and drinks and the gas tanks are full." He hands me an envelope and continues, "Here are the coordinates of where we think the wreck is located. Give me a call me when you get back."

"You're not going along, Mr. Plum?" I quickly ask.

"Oh no, I get seasick just looking at the ocean."

The three unsavory characters load all of the equipment onboard. TC and I check out the GPS system on the boat. Everything seems to be working and the gas gauges read full. We head out to sea at about 11:30 with Mr. Plum and the dockhands waving goodbye. The temperature is 82 degrees, the sun is shining, and it's another beautiful day in paradise. The coordinates Mr. Plum gave us puts the wreck site about two miles off shore.

We are just moving along at a moderate pace, enjoying the weather when all of a sudden the engine begins to sputter about thirty minutes into our trip. TC shuts it down and I lift the engine compartment cover to see if I can figure out what's wrong. My Special Forces training kicks in, don't think, just react. I turn to TC and yell, "Jump TC, jump!" I take two broad strides and since he is just staring at me with a blank look on his face, I push him over the edge of the boat and dive in behind him. Just as we hit the water, the world around us explodes.

Chapter 68: Crowded in Antigua

It's Ginny Ridlinger's first full day in Antigua. Her goal is to find her old Air Force girlfriend, Moozie Cameron. She goes on Google and searches for the name of the bar she manages. Low and behold, there it is. She rents a car and heads out to find the address. As soon as she walks in the front door, she spots a familiar figure standing behind the bar. Their eyes meet at the same time, "Oh, my God, Ginny Ridlinger."

"Oh, my God, Moozie Cameron, and oh, my God, you've grown!"

Moozie laughs, "Not really," as she steps down from the six-inch step she had installed behind the full length of the bar so her 5'2" body could see over it.

She runs around the end of the bar and jumps up on Ginny. For about five minutes neither one stops talking. Finally Moozie asks, "Where are you staying and how long are you going to be here?"

"I'm staying at the Jolly Beach Resort and I'll be here for about two weeks."

"Well, you just go back and check out. You're moving in with me. I have a spare room and it's yours."

Moozie gives Ginny the address and tells her how to get there. She then puts the assistant manager in charge of the bar and goes home to spiff up the condo.

Ginny arrives about 11:30 and after some lunch and a bunch of small talk, they sit out on the screened-in porch facing the ocean. Moozie fixes Ginny a Rum Runner and fixes herself a Sex on the Beach. Life could not be less complicated than right now, just two old friends gazing at the ocean with a drink in their hand, reminiscing about old times.

They both notice the fireball at the same time and hear the dull explosion seconds later. Ginny looks at Moozie and says, "My God, what was that?"

"I don't know, but if it was a boat, whoever was on board is probably dead."

❧◦◦❧

That same morning Beverly and Rick are flying into Antigua. They had been in the Virgin Islands the day before checking out some Stephanie sightings, which turned out to be a wild goose chase. Since most of her calls have been from Antigua, they came here to check out some of those leads.

Beverly is daydreaming while staring out of the plane's window at a small boat below. She has been watching it splash across the ocean but then it abruptly goes dead in the water. All of a sudden, all hell breaks loose and the boat literally blows up right in front of her. She motions to Rick, who is preparing for their final ascent into the airport, to go down and take a look. He banks the plane in the direction Beverly was pointing and sees the fire and smoke. He makes a low pass and they notice two people in the water. He tips his wings to signify they see them and will send help. He gets on his radio and calls the emergency channel to report the problem and the location. As they are proceeding to the airport, they notice a boat speeding toward the scene of the accident. Rick says to Beverly, "Looks like help is on the way."

Rick's so-called "help" is a speedboat with Mr. Plum and his three dockhands, and they all have weapons at the ready.

❧◦◦❧

Dr. Jon Spineback and Mary Jo are sitting on the beach drinking Bloody Marys when they hear the sound of the explosion and notice the smoke plume out in the ocean.

Dr. Jon has been checking online to see the status of the Stuart Peterson case. So far, so good. His name has not been mentioned. He is considering flying back to the mainland to make sure his monthly pain pill junkies get their fix, check on his house, and pick up some more cash. However, after much thought, he just gets online and transfers money from his Columbus account to a bank in Antigua. He figures he is in the clear so far since the money transfer goes through with no problem.

Stephanie Langchester is also on the beach. She is wearing sunglasses and a large sun hat. She is trying to decide if she should return to Georgetown and resume her search for Captain Swinely's buried treasure, and she is also wondering why Beverly is searching for her. She can't believe the authorities have any idea she was involved with the death of the lowlifes in Charleston. She did speak with her contact and close friend at British Intelligence who does not know where she is located, and he said they have two operatives in the Caribbean looking for her. He tells her the scuttlebutt around the office is that they also hired a private firm to search for her as well. If that's true, she wonders if Beverly is part of that search.

Stephanie has spent the last couple of days picking up Beverly's flyers and disposing of them. She usually wears a wig and inconspicuous clothing so as not to draw any undue attention. She is glad Beverly did not mention her height on the flyers. That would be a dead giveaway. She removes her glasses and raises her hat when she hears the remnants of the explosion and sees the smoke.

Chapter 69: Evidence

Detective Reynolds has been busy lately. He received his long-awaited warrant to search Stuart Peterson's office and apartment. He has also finally found out where he thinks Dr. Jon Spineback and his wife went on vacation. Since he couldn't find them at the Columbus International Airport, he started searching local private airports. He found what he was looking for when he checked out Don Scott Field. Dr. Spineback had booked a private flight to Key West, not Canada, and that led him to another private flight from Key West to Antigua. He finds the Doctor's black SUV located in the long-term parking lot at the airport. He tries to call Mickke D; however, his cell phone keeps going to voicemail.

He and his forensic crew enter Stuart Peterson's computer store about the same time as another crew enters Mr. Peterson's apartment. Both crews are looking for anything that might tie Mr. Peterson to Dr. Jon Spineback and/or his twin brother Von.

At the shop, they end up taking three laptops and two computers. They also take several thumb drives they find in different locations in the shop. Now it will be up to the forensic people to see what they can find on the computers, laptops, and thumb drives.

At Stuart Peterson's apartment, they find two more laptops and five thumb drives. One they found taped under a drawer in his desk. They also confiscated several thousands of dollars in cash, assault rifles, shotguns, and three handguns.

Detective Reynolds puts a rush on everything they have discovered. He needs proof that Stuart was working for one or both of the Spineback twins. Once back in the office, he tries to call Mickke D again. The call goes to voicemail as before.

Chapter 70: The Colombians

TC and I both pop to the surface of the debris-scattered ocean at about the same time. We hear the plane and watch it skim the ocean and tip its wings, as we frantically wave.

Somehow, the boat is still afloat, or at least the front half of the boat is still above water. We grab hold to steady ourselves. I look at TC and say, "Do you still think I'm paranoid?"

"What the hell was that? Thanks for the push. Are you OK?" he asks while gasping for air.

"I'm OK but I'm not sure we're out of the woods yet," as I turn and point. "That boat coming our way could be a friend or possibly a foe. At least the plane that just flew over knows we're here."

TC replies, "Well, if it's a foe, we're sitting ducks."

"No shit, TC." I notice an air tank rolling around on what's left of the boat deck. "TC, grab those masks and that air supply line floating over there and I'll try to snatch that air tank. Maybe we can stay submerged until we determine their intentions."

I am hoping the air tank is undamaged and the supply line works. I raise myself up on the deck and drag the air tank over the edge just as a spray of bullets smash into the deck. "TC, I'm pretty sure it's not a friend."

We quickly hook up the supply line to the tank. At least for now there are air bubbles coming out. We fill our lungs with air and dive just as Mr. Plum and his dockhands arrive. They pepper the ocean with bullets, which pass harmlessly around us.

TC has the air tank strapped to his back and we keep sharing its life-giving resource. I can see the shadow of the newly arrived boat about thirty feet above us and they keep sending bullets our way. I finally decide it's time to fish or cut bait. I motion to TC to keep moving around down here and that I am going up. His eyes widen but he nods his head.

I fill my lungs with air and slowly float up. I stay under and to the rear of the boat's shadow. I surface, take a big gulp of real air, and grab hold of the swim platform at the rear of the boat. I fetch my trusty .45 from its holster in the small of my back, and shake it out of the water to dry it off. I can hear the rifles firing into the water at TC.

The decisive moment has arrived. I hoist myself up on the platform and say, "Hey, you guys looking for me?" As they turn to the sound of my voice, I fire three times, pop, pop, pop, and the three dockhands fall. Mr. Plum is staring at me with a handgun hanging at his side. "Go ahead Mr. Plum, make my day." He drops the gun on the deck.

I climb on board and walk over to Mr. Plum. I pick up his gun and put it in my waistband. I take my foot and shove the assault rifles away from the fallen dockhands. "Who sent you to kill me, Mr. Plum?"

"I want a lawyer," he stammers.

I smash my fist into his nose and reply, "Wrong answer." He falls to the deck as blood spews from his broken nose and decorates his white suit with red polka dots. Just then, I hear and notice movement from the rear of the boat. I quickly turn with gun in hand, and there is TC.

As I help him onboard, he says, "Sorry, Mickke D, the tank ran out of air. Must have been a leak somewhere. Looks like you have this situation under control."

"For now, find something to tie your friend's hands with. He is not cooperating."

I turn as two other boats approach our location. One looks like a search and rescue and the other is a Royal Police Force boat. I wave their way and lay my weapon and Mr. Plum's gun on the deck.

There are three local police officers on the police boat and they come onboard. As soon as they see the dockhands lying on the deck and weapons strewn about, they draw their weapons. I suppose their first thought is this is a drug deal gone badly. TC and

I raise our hands and Mr. Plum blurts out, "Arrest them, they shot my friends and attacked me. We came over to help them."

One of the officers looks at me and asks, "What happened to him?" Pointing at the trembling Mr. Plum.

I reply, "He fell down and hit his nose."

We all turn, as there is a loud swishing sound as our boat finally succumbs to the explosion and sinks into the clear blue-green sea.

The same officer asks, "What happened to that boat?"

"These people tried to kill us by blowing up our boat," pointing at the dockhands and Mr. Plum.

"That's absurd," Mr. Plum replies, holding his nose.

The police officer motions for the search and rescue boat to pull alongside and two men come on board to look after the dockhands and Mr. Plum. They proclaim one of the dockhands as deceased. They load the wounded and the dead guy onto the search and rescue boat along with one policeman, while TC, Mr. Plum, and I return to the island, along with all of the weapons, in the police boat. They hook up Mr. Plum's boat and tow it behind.

We spend the next two hours explaining our side of the story to an inspector with the Royal Police Force and I assume they did background checks on us with Interpol. We give a written statement and turn over our passports. They don't want us leaving the island until they have this whole thing figured out. They tend to Mr. Plum's nose and lock him up. I guess they did a background check on him as well. I ask for my .45; however, they tell me I can retrieve it when I get my passport back.

TC and I don't mind. We have our rooms and rental car paid for by Mr. Plum and $25,000 in cash to spend, although $1,000 of that may be a little bit soggy. Life is good. Now maybe I can finally get in some R & R.

Just as we are walking out of the station, my cell phone rings. I stop to answer, thanks to the waterproof case on my phone. The call is from big Steve. "I have more good news for you. Are you sitting down?"

"Trust me big Steve, you can't make my day any worse than it already is." I figure I can get by calling him big Steve since he is in Lancaster.

He pauses before answering, "Well, digest this. Dr. Jon Spineback is also in Antigua along with his wife."

I was wrong. My day can get worse and a lot more complicated. "You have to be kidding me. Is Ohio running a special to Antigua? Are you sure Von Spineback is not here as well?"

"No, he's still here. We have him under 24/7 surveillance. Why has your day been so bad? I thought you were there for some R & R?"

"Well, someone blew up the boat we were on."

He chuckles, "You seem to have a problem with things blowing up around you. Was it some woman's husband?"

"Very funny. Keep me advised when the rest of Ohio heads my way. I'll keep my eyes peeled for Ginny Ridlinger and now Dr. Jon as well."

Just as we are about to leave through the sliding glass doors at the police station, I grab TC and pull him back inside. I can't believe my eyes. Walking up the sidewalk toward the police station is my ex-girlfriend Beverly and some guy who looks familiar to me. "TC, sneak a look at that woman coming up the walk. Do you recognize her?"

He peeks around the corner, "My God, Mickke D, she looks like Beverly."

"Thanks. I was beginning to think that explosion screwed up my vision."

"Who's the guy with her?"

"Damn, now I remember. That's Rick! He's a pilot I met not too long ago."

"Don't you want to say hello? I thought she was your girlfriend."

"No, ex-girlfriend." We vanish around the corner as they pass by.

I am having mixed thoughts about seeing Beverly. My heart and body is telling me it would sure be nice to spend some quality time with her but my brain is telling me she could be a stone-cold killer. I'm not sure which part is going to win out.

ఎక్ర

Later, as we are walking into our hotel, TC bends down to pick up a piece of paper in the grass. He's big on litter control. He looks at it and says, "Oh, my God, look at this."

I take the flyer and say, "You have got to be kidding me, that's Stephanie, is she here also? I thought you said you saw her in Georgetown?"

TC replies, "No, I said I *thought* I saw her in Georgetown."

I get my phone and dial the number on the flyer. A woman answers, "This is Cathy, how may I help you?"

I am stunned speechless, but quickly recover and sternly respond, "We need to talk."

Beverly hesitates, and then hangs up.

I know it is Beverly, I recognize her voice. My life is turning into a zoo. I am going to need a referee and a scorekeeper to keep track of all of the players. Beverly, Rick, Stephanie, Dr. Jon, and Ginny Ridlinger. I wonder who else is going to show up? In addition, here I am without a weapon.

Things continue to go downhill. When we walk into TC's room, we can't believe our eyes. The place has been ransacked. Someone was looking for something. It is a good thing TC put the briefcase with the $24,000 in the hotel safe. We both look at each other at the same time. He calls the front desk and they confirm the briefcase is still there. I go over to my room and it also has been turned upside down.

I know it couldn't have been Mr. Plum and his crew; they were trying to kill us at the time, so who else would know we had the money, if that's what they were looking for?

ఎక్ర

It actually was Mr. Plum. He had hired two local hoodlums to get the briefcase back while they were at the marina. Mr. Plum, when registering, had asked for a second key to both rooms. He called after TC and Mickke D left the marina on the salvage boat. The only problem was that a surveillance camera showed the two men entering each room. The Royal Police Force had both men in custody within two hours of our call about the break in. They both confessed after being shown the tape and a picture of Mr. Plum.

Chapter 71: Ginny is Surprised

Ginny and Moozie finish their second drink and decide to take a couple of chairs and journey over to the beach for some catching up in the sun. Also, they think maybe someone there will know something about that explosion. They opt to take iced tea with them this time instead of booze. They find a nice sunny location not far from the water where they talk for about thirty minutes and mutually agree that maybe it's time for a power nap.

Ginny closes her eyes for not more than five minutes when she, for some unknown reason, opens them again. Her eyes widen. There, walking on the beach not twenty feet in front of her is a man, who looks exactly like Von Spineback. He's with some woman she has never seen. Thankfully, they do not look her way. She crosses her legs and pulls her borrowed sun hat down over her eyes.

All of a sudden, she decides it might be nice to breathe, and she gasps for air, which wakes up Moozie. "I think I'm ready to head back to the condo Moozie, I need to pee."

"Yeah, me too. Hey, are you allright?" Moozie asks.

"I'm good, just had a quick nightmare."

On their walk back to the condo, Ginny asks, "Say Moozie, do you own a gun?"

"A gun, hell I own three handguns, an assault rifle, and a shotgun. Do you want to go down to the range and burn off some magazines?"

"No, but I wonder if I could borrow one of your handguns while I'm here. I always carried back in the States, and I'm beginning to feel naked without one."

"Well girlfriend, I certainly don't want you running around naked. I've got a snub nose .38 that will fit great in your purse."

"Thanks Moozie, I feel safer already."

Many thoughts are running through Ginny's head. She can't believe she may have just seen Von and if it was him, why would he be in Antigua and who was that woman walking with him? Should she call him? If she does, and it wasn't him, then he may find out where she is, and that would not be a good thing. On the other hand, if it was him, that would even be a worse thing.

Chapter 72: Beverly and Rick

Beverly and Rick land safely at the airport. They immediately check with the tower on the status of the two people they saw waving next to the exploded boat. They are told that two men were picked up just minutes ago and both appear to be unhurt. They are also told that the local police would like to speak with them since they were witnesses to the explosion.

They grab a quick lunch, make some calls on Stephanie sightings, pass out some more flyers, and then about mid-afternoon go to the police station to give their statements. Beverly is hesitant; she is not sure it is a good idea. She knows her identity is solid but she's not sure about Rick. He assures her he is clean and will pass muster.

As they walk through the sliding glass doors into the Royal Police Force station, Beverly has one of those strange feelings that someone or something is just not right. She looks around and sees nothing that alarms her.

They meet with the inspector in charge of the boat explosion and he asks some rather simple questions and takes their statements. Rick asks if they have identified the two people in the water and if they are okay.

The inspector replies, "Both of them seem to be fine. They are from Myrtle Beach, in the States, a Mr. Cadium and a Mr. Mac-Candlish, who is a private investigator. They were here for a possible salvage operation. They are both lucky to be alive."

Even though she is sitting down, Beverly feels weak in the knees and steadies herself against her chair. Rick asks with a frown on his face, "What were their first names?"

The inspector opens a file folder and replies, "One of them was Thomas and the other one's name was Mickke. Why, do you know them? They just left about ten minutes before you came in."

Beverly now knows where her odd feeling came from.

"No, I guess not. Are you ready? "He asks, looking at a flush-faced Beverly.

As they move toward the door, the inspector asks, "By the way, why are you two in Antigua?"

They both stop dead in their tracks and look at each other. Beverly snaps back to attention. She returns to where the inspector is standing, gives him her biggest smile, and pulls out a flyer from her purse. As she hands it to him, she says, "I'm looking for my missing sister. If you see her, please let me know."

Once outside, Rick turns to Beverly, "You're not going to believe this, but the guy named Mickke is the same guy I met in Colombia and the same person who told me about Myrtle Beach."

"That's great Rick, I'm happy for you. Now let's get the hell out of here."

Chapter 73: Mr. Fredrick

Detective Reynolds is finally having a good day. His forensic people found information on the thumb drive that they found taped under one of the desk drawers in Mr. Peterson's apartment. It seems as if Stuart Peterson wanted to keep track of his escapades. It contained a complete list of what seems to be Stuart's clients, targets, and payments received. The list of clients included a Fredrick, a Jon, and a Von. The only problem is that the targets have no names. They seem to be noted by initials and there are no last names of his clients: Von – SA = $25,000. Jon – AC = $500. Fredrick – DR = $10,000. The list contains fifteen entries and Officer Frederick seems to have been his best client. They will now need to check into any unsolved killings in the central Ohio area and see if any of the names match the initials. Detective Reynolds wonders if SA stands for Sissy Adams?

He contacts the District Attorney and asks for an opinion. He is told the real problem is that none of it will stand up in court because there are no last names and the initials and first names could belong to anyone. And, the biggest concern is that Stuart Peterson is dead. He is told he will probably need confessions.

Detective Reynolds opts to interrogate Mr. Fredrick again. His attorney is present. "Mr. Fredrick, we found a thumb drive in Stuart Peterson's apartment and your name was listed on it with a lot of other names along with payments to Mr. Peterson. What is that about?"

The attorney answers, "Could I have a copy of that, detective?"

"We are still analyzing it at this time, but I'll get you a copy when we're finished. And again," looking back at Mr. Fredrick, "tell me why you were up on Mt. Pleasant that morning with an assault rifle, Mr. Fredrick."

Mr. Fredrick just glares at Detective Reynolds and his attorney answers again, "Detective we've been through this before. My client just happened to be driving by when he heard what sounded like gunshots coming from the top of the mountain. Being a law-abiding person with a security background, he decided to help out with a possible problem."

"And why did he have an assault rifle with him?"

"He opened his trunk and grabbed the first weapon he saw."

Detective Reynolds continues, "And why did he say 'he should have shot him when he had a chance'?"

"Detective, had you read my client his rights before you possibly heard him say that? No, you didn't, so it won't be admissible in court. Now, is there anything else? I think we're finished here."

As they are getting up to leave, Mr. Frederick pounds his fist on the table and yells at Detective Reynolds. "You know what, detective? If the police did their job and got all of these drug dealers, dope heads, and pimps off the streets, I would not have to hire people like Stuart Peterson to do it."

His attorney grabs his arm and yells out, "Be quiet! Don't say another word."

Mr. Fredrick does not obey. "I had some very good friends killed in a drive-by shooting where the shooters got the wrong address. Did the police find out who did it? No, but I did, and now they will never go to the wrong address, or any address, again."

Detective Reynolds jumps into the ruckus, "Well, Mr. Fredrick, why didn't you tell the police what you found and allow the justice system to do its job?"

"Because even if they were convicted, they would just spend life in jail and we the taxpayers would be paying for it."

Detective Reynolds says, "Well, Mr. Fredrick, let me ask you this, you say the shooters got the wrong address. What if you found the wrong shooters and had the wrong people killed?"

Mr. Fredrick starts to answer but then shuts up as two police officers arrive. Detective Reynolds tells them to take Mr. Fredrick away. "Counselor, your client is being charged with intent to commit murder."

❧

Next on Detective Reynolds' list of things to do is to arrest Von Spineback. He knows it won't stick at this point in time but he wants to rattle his cage a little bit. He needs to get him in Fairfield County to serve the arrest warrant so he goes out to the company's temporary office, a doublewide mobile home on West Fair Avenue. He tells the only person there, a geologist named Foreman, to call Von and tell him there is a problem and to get here as soon as possible. He has Mr. Foreman hang up before Von can ask any questions. Von arrives about 30 minutes later. Detective Reynolds is waiting for him. "Mr. Spineback, I have a warrant for your arrest. Cuff him, Turtle, and read him his rights."

Von Spineback has a confused look on his face. "What are you arresting me for? I need to call my attorney."

"In due time Mr. Spineback, in due time."

Von looks back as he goes out the door and says, "Foreman, you're fired."

Chapter 74: Liz

Liz Woodkark has been doing her due diligence on Beverly's case. She has discovered that the three men who bought TC's boat from the three women, who Stephanie supposedly killed, have all been murdered. The only witnesses say it was a woman. It seems as if no one, including British Intelligence, has put two and two together, which seems strange to her. She checks into the relatives of the murdered women and no one stands out as a cold-blooded revenge killer. That leaves Stephanie. However, if Stephanie had killed the girls, then why kill the men? However, if she somehow found out the men had killed the girls, then Stephanie would have a possible revenge motive.

She calls Beverly and tells her to back off for now but to stay in the area. Beverly wishes she had told her to come home. That would solve one big problem, the possibility of running into TC or Mickke D. She opts not to tell Liz about them being in Antigua.

Chapter 75: Time to Leave

I awake to a bolt of lightning flashing across the open curtain window in my room, followed by a crash of thunder. The clock on the stand by my bed reads 4:15 in bright red digital numbers. I was having one of my bad nightmares so the early morning wake-up call is welcome. Since I do not want to fall back into the nightmare mode, I get up, go to the bathroom, and get a drink of water. I sit in the dark in a comfortable chair while staring out the window watching Mother Nature's fireworks display with vivid sound effects.

My thoughts keep going back to Beverly. What is she doing in Antigua and why was Rick with her? I figure he does contract work for the military and the CIA, so maybe that's the connection. I don't want to believe she killed Terry Graf in Myrtle Beach, but I know everything points to her. Also, I've seen her in action on the Boardwalk. She was well-trained by someone.

I must have dozed off, because the next thing I know, its 7:00 and I have a crick in my neck. I shower and meet TC for breakfast at 8:00. At 8:30, my phone rings. It's the inspector from the Royal Police Force. He tells me we have been cleared and we can pick up our passports and my .45 anytime. I relay the message to TC and we decide to go directly to the police station and get our passports and my weapon.

❧❧

The inspector tells us after Interpol checked into Mr. Plum's background, they discovered he was Colombian and close friends of the Valdez cartel family. With that information and the confession from the two men who sacked our rooms, Mr. Plum will be in jail for a long time.

We thank the inspector, take our passports and my weapon, and start to leave the station. The inspector calls out, "Oh, I forgot to tell you, there was a man and woman in here, right after you left the other day, who I think knows you. A woman named Cathy and her friend Rick. Do you know them?"

I look at TC, turn, and answer, "Sorry, names don't ring a bell, but thanks for letting us know."

We begin to leave again and the inspector asks, "By the way, what was in the briefcase the two men were looking for?"

Again, I look at TC. He responds, "Oh, just some paperwork and maps pertaining to a possible salvage job."

He smiles at us and says, "Enjoy your visit to Antigua, gentlemen. I trust you will be leaving our beautiful island before long?"

We wave, turn, and leave the building. Once outside, I say to TC, "I think I've had enough fun, what do you say we take the inspector's advice and head back to Myrtle Beach?"

"I was thinking the same thing. I'll make the arrangements this afternoon. Maybe it's time to start looking for Captain Swinely's buried treasure again."

He's thinking about buried treasure and I am thinking to myself that I hope I don't have to make another trip to Colombia.

Chapter 76: Von is Out

Von Spineback calls his attorney and is out on bail the same afternoon he is arrested by Detective Reynolds. They charged him with conspiring to commit murder. That was the good news. Things begin going downhill for Von after that. The arrest sets in motion a series of high-level meetings at Wilmont Oil & Gas Company that end with Von being relieved of his position as president of the company. He is offered a very small buyout package and he has to divest himself of all of his interest in the wells he has invested in which were already drilled in Fairfield County. The company is having enough public relations problems without their president accused of ordering the killing of a local reporter. Von is given two hours to clean out his office, turn in his keys, and leave the building.

Von is devastated. He had planned everything so well and if it had all come together, he would be set for life. Now, he has to prepare for his day in court. He realizes they don't have much of a case against him. He knows of only three possible witnesses who could bring him down: Ginny Ridlinger, Robert Dane, and his secretary Marian. Each of them knows of a connection between him and Stuart Peterson although probably only circumstantial. If they don't testify, he is free and clear.

❧❦

After the price of oil hits rock bottom, Wilmont Oil & Gas decides to sell all of their interest in the Fairfield County project for a nice profit and over-rides. The purchase of the Anchor Hocking Distribution Center is no longer on the table.

Chapter 77: Ginny and Dr. Jon

The day after seeing who she thought was Von Spineback on the beach, Ginny and Moozie decide to have lunch at an outdoor deli close to Moozie's condo. They have been having a great time catching up on each other's past lives, but Ginny can't get Von out of her mind. She placed Moozie's .38 in her purse yesterday and it is still there. She can't decide if she wants to go back to Lancaster or take her chances here in Antigua with Moozie, who has offered her a job and a place to live.

Von has called her every day at least once since she left town and she just allows the call to go to voicemail and then deletes it. She remembers that Von spent a lot of time with Stuart and he always said how much he admired the way Stuart got things done. He never left any loose ends. She truthfully believes that he would do whatever it takes to keep from going to jail. That could mean getting rid of all witnesses, which includes her.

They both have a cobb salad for lunch and split a bottle of wine. They then opt to take a stroll on the beach to justify the wine. After about ten minutes, Ginny suddenly stops and says to Moozie, "Oh, my God, get ready to call 911."

"What are you talking about, girlfriend? Why would I call 911?"

Ginny has spotted the man from yesterday who she thinks is Von Spineback coming their way and he is alone this time. He is looking directly at her with a tight smile that seems more like a smirk to Ginny. She panics and draws her weapon from her purse.

Dr. Jon, who told Mary Jo to relax and spend the day at the spa, is actually trolling the beach looking for some young innocent girl to share an afternoon fling. He can't believe his eyes when he sees this woman draw a gun and point it at him. All he did was smile at her. With a bewildered look on his face he says, "What's wrong with you lady, are you crazy?" He looks around and says to no one in particular, "Someone call the police."

"I'm not crazy, you're the crazy one. Why did you follow me to Antigua?" She yells as complete human silence envelopes the beach area around them. The only sounds are coming from the ocean.

Dr. Jon remembers he has his weapon tucked in his waistband covered by a long beach shirt. "I don't know who you think I am, but let me get my driver's license out of my back pocket to show you." He reaches behind, grabs his wallet with his left hand and pulls his gun with his right hand. He points it at Ginny. "Drop your gun, lady, or I'll blow you away."

The scene looks like a duel from an old movie. They are twenty feet apart and pointing guns at each other. "You bastard," she exclaims as she pulls the trigger.

Dr. Jon pulls his trigger at exactly the same time. Witnesses swear they only heard one shot.

Ginny and Dr. Jon fall to their knees and crumble on the sandy beach. Both shots are fatal. Dr. Jon had no idea who Ginny was and Ginny had no idea it was Jon Spineback and not Von.

Chapter 78: Shots Fired

TC and I have just finished having lunch and are walking toward our vehicle when I flinch as we hear the unmistakable sound of a gunshot. It seems to have come from the beach, so we walk quickly in that direction. When we arrive, there is a small crowd milling around and yelling for someone to call for an ambulance. I push my way through and I see two bodies sprawled face up on the beach. Their eyes are open but not seeing. Blood is oozing from their lifeless remains. The tide is washing away their blood and carrying it out to sea. I look closely and can't believe my eyes. It's Ginny Ridlinger and Dr. Jon Spineback.

Just then, the police arrive, and it's the inspector who not so long ago suggested we leave town. He looks at us and says, "Tell me you two had nothing to do with this."

"Not us inspector, we just got here. However, I can tell you who they are."

An ambulance arrives next, declares them dead, and takes the bodies away. I fill the inspector in with names and the fact that both of them were suspects in several murders back in Ohio. He tells us to come back down to the station and give a written statement.

He asks if anyone in the crowd witnessed the shooting and several people raise their hands, including Moozie. The shock of seeing her friend killed right in front of her made her knees weak. She is sitting on the sand with her head in her hands.

ॐॐ

Before heading back to the police station, I call big Steve, "Detective, you're not going to believe what just happened here in Antigua."

"Mickke D, if you're involved, trust me, I will not be surprised."

I ask, "First of all, are you sure Von Spineback is still in Ohio?"

"Absolutely, he's being watched 24/7. I just had an update about thirty minutes ago. Why do you ask?"

"Because Ginny Ridlinger and Dr. Jon Spineback are both dead. Looks like they shot each other right here on the beach in broad daylight."

"What? I didn't know they even knew each other."

"I doubt if they did. I'm guessing Ginny thought Dr. Jon was Von. Maybe they had a falling out and that's why she left town. Maybe she panicked when she thought he was here in Antigua."

After a slight hesitation, he replies, "And you were not involved in any way?"

"Absolutely not. We got there after the shooting and I identified the bodies for the local police."

"Let's see, your boat gets blown up, you shoot three Colombians, and now two people you know kill each other on the beach. I can't believe they haven't deported you by now."

"That's not funny. I think that is about to happen. The police have suggested we go back to the States. Can I use you as a reference?"

Detective Reynolds hangs up without answering. I say into an empty cell phone, "Thanks, detective, I always take no as a definite maybe."

Chapter 79: The Confrontation

Stephanie Langchester also heard the gunshot. In full disguise, she ventures down to the beach to see what is going on. She stays back and surveys the crowd before moving forward. She watches as two men enter the area. She is stunned. She immediately recognizes them as Mickke D and TC. She stares in disbelief. This small island is all of a sudden becoming very crowded.

As she turns to leave, she quickly turns back around and bends down to fiddle with one of her flip-flops. Her heartbeat increases and she reaches into her purse to be sure her gun is available. She holds her breath as Beverly and that same guy she was with before pass by. She watches as Beverly says something to her companion and they exit away from the commotion on the beach.

Beverly and Rick were walking by and heard the shot. They venture toward the crowd. Beverly noticed Mickke D and TC among the onlookers at the shooting site. She tells Rick they need to put up more flyers and make some more calls. She needs to get him away from there before he recognizes Mickke D and causes a major embarrassment and possibly a dangerous situation.

For some unknown reason, she glances to her left and notices a tall, dark-haired woman wearing sunglasses turning to walk away from the scene. Tension fills her body and her palms begin to sweat. She touches her clutch bag and feels the shape of her weapon. She says to Rick, "Stop walking but don't look around. I think I just spotted my long-lost sister."

Rick gives her a big grin. "Really. Is that good or bad?"

"Well, if she's packing, it could be bad." She continues, "I'm going to confront her and I need you to watch my back. I also want her to see you."

"Okay MB, it's your rodeo, but I get paid more for being in a combat zone."

❧❦

Stephanie walks away from the scene on the beach and just as she reaches a small grove of trees, she hears someone calling her name, "Stephanie, how are you? I haven't seen you since Myrtle Beach."

Rick, who is looping around while keeping Stephanie in his sights, stops and says to himself, *I thought she said she had never been in Myrtle Beach?*

Stephanie turns and sees Beverly walking toward her and her friend coming at her from her right. "I'm sorry, you must have me confused with someone else. My name is Sista not Stephanie."

"Sista my ass," Beverly says as she stops and puts her hand in her purse. Stephanie puts her hand in her purse and Rick reaches for his weapon.

❧❦

TC and I are about to leave the beach when I take one last look around and see a scary scene. Near a small grove of trees, I notice three familiar-looking people, two women and one man, in what looks like a tense situation. I tell TC to stay here but to be ready to call for help if needed. I start walking towards the trio and my worst fears are confirmed. It's Stephanie Langchester, Beverly, and Rick, and they are not getting ready for a group hug. It looks to me like all three have their hand on a weapon.

There are quite a few civilians and the police within a stone's throw. This has all the makings for a bad ending. All three turn as

I walk up and say, "How y'all doing? How come I wasn't invited to the party?"

Rick, still grinning, is the only one who answers, "Mickke D, it's Rick from Colombia, how are you?"

Before I can reply and unexpectedly, Stephanie says looking at Rick, "Do you grin all the time?"

Beverly replies, "Yes, he does. I think it's an affliction he has with his face."

That banter seems to have dropped the anxiety level within the group. I notice all three of them lessen the grip on their unseen weapons and their shoulders drop just a dab, another sign that their bodies are relaxing a wee bit. I need to defuse this situation as soon as possible.

"Look guys, there are a lot of innocent civilians and police with guns nearby, so let's discuss whatever problem you seem to be having with each other in a civil manner."

None of the three respond. I continue, "First of all, everyone please take your hand off of your weapon. This is not the O.K. Corral. If you want to kill each other, do it somewhere quiet and secluded."

I now see two hands visible from each of them. All of a sudden, the group's anxiety level goes back up. The crime scene inspector walks up to us and says, "Mr. MacCandlish, don't forget, I need you and Mr. Cadium down at my office right away. Oh, I see you ran into the friends you didn't seem to know!"

"That's right inspector, once I saw their faces, I remembered their names. Small world, isn't it?"

With a frown on his face he replies, "I expect you in my office in thirty minutes."

"Yes sir, we'll be there."

The inspector turns and leaves the area and as he passes TC, he says something. TC nods his head. I turn back to the group. "I am going to ask some questions and then as soon as you answer you can all go on your merry way."

Stephanie says in a defiant tone of voice, "And who put you in charge?"

Sternly I reply, "I did and I'm going to start with you. Why did you steal TC's boat and all of the artifacts from *The Queen Beth*?"

She pauses and then answers, "That was going to be our retirement fund and I figured TC's boat was insured anyway. We didn't harm anyone. It was a victimless crime."

"Victimless crime, what about the other three girls? Who killed them?"

"Well, it certainly wasn't me."

"What about the three guys who purchased TC's stolen boat and were later found murdered? Witnesses said the killer was a woman."

"Don't know anything about that but you know what, maybe they did something wrong and deserved to die. Anything else, Mr. man-in-charge?"

I turn my attention to Beverly. "So Beverly, why are you in Antigua, why are you looking for Stephanie, why is Rick with you, and why did you leave Myrtle Beach in such a big hurry?"

Beverly was thinking of answers as Mickke D was throwing questions at Stephanie. She is ready, "I was hired by an insurance company to try and find the artifacts which were stolen from *The Queen Beth*. Seems like the State of South Carolina insured everything Stephanie's crew and TC salvaged. So of course, I started with Stephanie. I hired Rick because I needed a pilot and an airplane to find her. I left Myrtle Beach because I needed a vacation. Anything else?"

I look at Rick who is still grinning, "That's right, Mickke D. She needed an airplane and a pilot. I had no idea she knew you. By the way, I'm looking at a bar up your way. I'll give you a call when I get up there."

I look at all of them with a "what a bunch of liars" look on my face. I turn without saying anything and walk away, hoping above all that I don't hear gunfire. Once I reach TC and look around, they have vanished.

☙❧

Stephanie looks at Beverly and says, "So where do we go from here and who are you working for?"

"If I told you that, I would have to kill you." Beverly thinks for a few seconds, makes a major decision, and continues, "As far as I'm concerned, I never found you. And, if you didn't kill your three friends, I could care less what happened to the guys who had TC's boat. Let's go Rick, we're out of here."

They slowly back away from each other and go their separate ways. Beverly looks hard at Rick and says, "Rick, if you know what's good for you, this meeting never took place."

Along with his continuing grin, he answers, "You got it Scary Mary, or MB, or Beverly, or Cathy, or whoever you are. I was never here."

કર્જ

Donna and Sam are watching the entire episode from across the street. When the group disperses, Sam says to Donna, "Call the boss and tell him the Yanks did not finish the job and ask him if we are to finish it for them."

કર્જ

TC and I spend about thirty minutes at the police station while I give the inspector a detailed report on Ginny Ridlinger and Dr. Jon Spineback. As we are getting ready to leave, he makes it quite clear we should leave the island ASAP. We both agree with him. Once we get back to the hotel, TC contacts the airline and they say they will pick us up at 11:00 in the morning.

We make it to the plane on time the next morning with no problems. We hear no news of anyone being shot and our friend the inspector is at the gate to wave goodbye. We arrive in Myrtle Beach that same afternoon.

Chapter 80: News from Ohio

It has been two months since I got back from Antigua. I've been burying myself in my work and have seriously considered writing a book. I've talked to several local authors in the area and they seem to think I have a great deal of first-hand research for a murder mystery whodunit, but I'm not sure writing is for me.

I've been in contact with big Steve and he has been keeping me updated on Von Spineback's trial. Two possible witnesses for the prosecution, Robert Dane and Von's secretary Marian, have disappeared. Big Steve seems to think there could be a mistrial or he may be found not guilty. The judge did allow my deposition to be placed into evidence, but again it was just considered hearsay. I offered to come back to testify in person, but I was told that would not be necessary.

I ask big Steve how Von could have gotten rid of witnesses if he had him tailed 24/7. His only reply is that maybe Von found himself another Stuart Peterson.

Chapter 81: Unexpected Visitor

It's around 7:30 in the evening and Blue and I have settled in for the night. I'm about half-asleep in my recliner and he is snoring and chasing rabbits on the couch. All of a sudden, I hear him growl and get off the couch. He heads to the front door. I reach for and find my .45 tucked under the table next to my chair. I slowly get up with gun in hand just as the doorbell rings. Blue is now whimpering and going crazy, not bad crazy but good crazy. He must know whoever is at the door. I relax and put my weapon in my waistband. I'm thinking it's Jim from next door, except he usually calls first.

I look out the side window and I am truly shocked. Standing on my stoop is Beverly. Blue starts to bark so I open the door.

She looks at me and says, "We need to talk."

We "talk" all night long.

Last Chapter

One month later, Liz Woodkark walks into a McDonald's just north of Atlanta. She orders a cup of coffee and takes a seat in a booth next to one of the exits. As she sips her coffee, she surveys the crowd and all of the customers coming in and going out. After about ten minutes, she sends a text on her phone. Five minutes later, Beverly enters the restaurant with a male companion. They order coffee and walk over to the booth where Liz awaits them. Beverly makes the introductions, "GG, this is Mickke D, Mickke D, this is GG."

Two days after my meeting with Beverly and GG, and a week after finding out that Von Spineback was found not guilty, I get a call from big Steve. "Mickke D, have you talked to Jake lately?"

"No, I haven't. Why do you ask?"

"Well, two days ago, he told his secretary that he was going to lunch and then he was going to climb the mountain for a little exercise. He never came back to the office. We found his car in the parking lot at Mt. Pleasant. We searched the mountain and the surrounding area and he is not there. I thought he may have called you."

A cold chill runs up and down my spine and the hairs on the back of my neck stand straight up. Should I tell him about the cave or should I wait and see if Jake shows up. Finally, I opt to tell him about the cave and to be careful.

He admonishes me and hangs up before I can explain.

My phone no more than touches my desk when it rings again. It's TC, and he is excited, "Mickke D, I think I may have found it!"

Excerpt from Steve's first book, *Murder on the Front Nine.*

I sluggishly and slowly pull myself out of bed around 7:00 AM. It's Saturday morning and I heard my overnight guest leave about 6:30. She told me last night she had to be at work by 7:00 at some resort on the ocean. She was a cute, well put together, young thing, with freckles, I'm guessing in her mid-twenties. I must have really made a big impression on her because she did not even say goodbye. She did leave a note which read, *Mickke D, been fun but my boyfriend will be back in town tomorrow. See ya "Pops".*

She never mentioned she had a boyfriend and what is this "pops" bit? Oh, well, there are quite a few available women in Myrtle Beach. Of course, sometimes I feel I have been married to most of them.

I walk into the bathroom and with blurry eyes gaze soulfully into the mirror. Staring back at me is a 45-year-old single again male about 6'1' 190 pounds with sandy blond hair. He looks to be in good shape when he sucks his stomach in and throws back his shoulders. Maybe not the buff, ex-Green Beret he was after mustering out of the Army fifteen years ago, but certainly not a "pops".

I throw on some shorts, a t-shirt, and flip-flops before going out to retrieve the morning paper. I smile as the warm, balmy, salt air hits my face. It looks like it is going to be another perfect day at the beach. I may even try to play golf today and forget about my rather mundane way of life here in Myrtle Beach.

That mundane way of life is about to change.

Excerpt from Steve's second book, *Cougars at the Beach.*

All at once I freeze. I spot him, maybe seventy-five yards in front of me, almost hidden by a large tree, watching me. Suddenly my adrenalin goes to high octane and the demons, which up to this point have only been hovering near the surface of my mind, begin to venture out.

He senses I have spotted him and he disappears behind the tree. I don't want to pull my weapon, have someone yell gun and start a stampede, so I take off at a brisk walk in his direction. Just past the last vendor, I break into a slow jog and I see him running toward the vineyard area and the parking lot. Just as I am about to start running after him, I notice a black streak come at me from my right side. I am completely surprised by the invasion, catch my foot on a root in the path. I stumble and fall head over heels on the ground. As I quickly rebound and get up on my hands and knees, I see the villain who attacked me. It is Starr, the vineyard dog, who must have thought I wanted to play with her. She is staring at me with both front legs on the ground, her rear end up in the air and tail wagging. I can tell by the look on her face she is thinking, *well, are you chasing me, or am I chasing you?*

DISCLOSURE

I tried to keep the descriptions of Mt. Pleasant as close to factual as possible. However, there is no secluded path leading to a forked tree and a cave. I made that up. My wife Beverly and I actually made a trip up the mountain to take pictures. We had not been up there in over twenty-five years. It is still a beautiful, awesome place.

Made in the USA
Columbia, SC
23 May 2018